The abolition of sadness

Walter Balerno

Table of contents

One

Solace awoke with grim difficulty to find himself in a colourful, well lit room. Lights reflected on the inside of the windows obscured his view of a dark grey exterior where towering structures emerged from a thick mist.

'Am I on a planet?'

'Yes. We made it.' Karla spoke gently, aware that Solace must feel terrible after being in stasis for decades. 'It was a tough slog and we lost some good people along the way but we made it.'

'The last thing I remember is talking to you on the Easy Rider. What happened?'

She knew she had to get straight to the point with Solace. 'You were depressed and editing yourself far too often. Lots of people were affected that way and suicide rates were high. We took a decision to put the worst affected in stasis until conditions improved. Now here we are.'

Solace looked out the window as a thick dirty sleet began to silently batter against it. 'Tell me the weather gets better than this.'

'We're on a planet, Solace. You can see sky, wander for hours in different places. You can even run around in the wilderness if you like. We're here to build a better world for ourselves.'

'So the weather here is always shit then,' he said with apparent resignation. 'How long was I in stasis?'

'We were in flight another sixty years and we've been here on Liszt for thirty.'

'Just thirty years. That means the climate has a long way to go before it gets anywhere close to pleasant. Why didn't you leave me under for longer?'

'It turns out that long term stasis isn't as safe as we thought. We had a few casualties so we just couldn't risk leaving people under any longer. Sorry to drag you back before we arrive at a more luxurious time!'

'I suppose it's better than death.' He sat upright in the bed. 'You look younger.'

'So do you. Medical technology has come a long way.'

'You made me younger? Without wrinkles how will people recognise my immense wisdom?'

She rolled her eyes. 'Sorry but it's not just about appearances. This planet would be tough on the elderly so we had to make sure you were robust. There's a bathroom there,' she pointed behind his bed. 'Why don't you take a shower then we can have a proper briefing?'

#

The grimy scrape of pink from a sun that wouldn't rise properly for months yet had long disappeared over the distant horizon and was entirely replaced by the diffuse glow of factory lights reflected off glowing clouds. Organs still functioned and blood still pumped, unaware of how little time remained. Her body was touched and explored as she lay there on the track expiring. Hands pulled down her pants and eyes looked. The use of her body continued after the organs finally ceased. She was left to cool rapidly in the gelid dark, piss dripping onto the stony ground, transporting some small parts of her on a journey as it washed downhill and froze. The things that had been her continued their exodus. Air she had breathed now drifted gently through the many other night vapours the planet had to offer. She extended some miles in many directions before discovery.

Gargantuan buildings embedded with tiny piercing lights rose up out of the rolling fog, their jutting angles naked one moment and hidden the next. A maintenance drone swam through the soupy atmosphere down towards FACT 10 where an obstruction had been detected by the train on Track 6.

#

Karla knew waking Solace had been a selfish act. He hadn't coped with being stuck on the Easy Rider and now here he was on a planet still in the early stages of development. She excused herself with the thought that at least here he could have solitude when he wanted it. And now, knowing his history, she could monitor him for signs of instability. She could have had a bracelet installed to monitor him properly but for some reason she couldn't pin down it was better that he didn't have one.

She touched her own bracelet as she walked quickly down the long curved corridor towards his room. She disliked the clumsy noise of her boots and wondered again how many years it would be until going outside no longer felt like an expedition requiring an adventurer's wardrobe. On Easy Rider she had enjoyed wandering barefoot on the gently warmed decks. Here she was always prepared for the harsh outdoors. Those years back on the ship had already taken on a historical hue. So much of her time there had been spent listening to ethereal music and reading books that it was like a long and tortuous holiday from reality. Here on Liszt the environment itself was enough to stop you dreaming. Liszt had more than its share of reality.

She arrived back at his room and entered without knocking.

'The good news is that my cock looks younger too,' said Solace as he came out of the bathroom searching for clothes.

Karla hadn't seen him naked for decades and now due to the rejuvenation process he looked younger than when they first met on the ship. It was the same lean physique but now he had a spring to his step. She felt proud for a moment, fondly imagining the adventures he might have now.

'Since you're on good form I might as well start your briefing with some fairly unappealing facts. First, as you may have guessed, a warm summer day here is minus fifteen.'

'Great.'

'But it's winter right now.'

'You're toying with me,' said Solace.

'In fact it's winter for the next few months.' She smiled and erupted into laughter. 'And that's just the weather.'

Solace watched her laugh but didn't join in. His sombre face made her a little embarrassed and the laughter wore off.

'We have problems here with mental health, addiction and violence. Things are going to be hard for decades to come and everybody knows it,' said Karla.

'Whatever happened to Easy Rider and our pioneering free spirit?'

'These people have already endured well over a century of shit.' She was annoyed that somebody who had barely lasted the first half-century on board, who had missed the worst of the journey, could question the achievement of even continuing to exist. 'You were asleep because you weren't tough enough.'

He nodded and bowed his head, as if to acknowledge his error of tact. 'Have we heard from any of the other ships?'

'Yes, some of them. There's a hardness to them. A frightening prospect for the societies they initiate. Some of them are still in flight, spraying micro fauna packages at unsuitable planets as they zip past.'

'Sounds like some of them may never stop. Space borne communities in endless exploration, afraid to face planetary life again.' Solace glazed over. 'You know waking up is hard. My thoughts feel as if they're underwater, damped by the slow music of a depressing future. I think my clock rate is reduced.'

'You always had such a melancholy taint to your imagination.' She felt his mood seep into her.

'Pensive and melancholy aren't the same thing,' he cautiously reminded her. 'Any news from Earth?'

She looked at him with something like loss, 'No contact since you took a long sleep.' Suddenly she felt as if he had left her in the lurch back then. Left her to cope with the difficult years and now his questions annoyed her. She tried hard to think of him as a fresh resource. When she looked down, she found his hand resting on hers.

'Can I suggest we continue this briefing later?' asked Solace.

'When I'm a little more acclimatised.'

'You don't even know where you live,' she said as he walked out the door. She remembered now his ability to annoy her.

\#

Outside figures looked like scratchy pencil lines with ill-defined hatching for shadows as the dense grey sleet wiped out all colour. Commuters even here, barely visible but for their suffering.

Solace stood still, heat slowly draining out of him, watching people pass by. There were few enough to pay attention to each for a few seconds without missing any out. A small energetic woman walking almost directly towards him returned his gaze for a little too long and he looked away, not wanting to be rude. A man who looked to be in his 30s but might be 200, walked close by wearing only boots, a t-shirt and trousers. His arms were like meat. The energetic woman seemed to become aware of his plight and looked around for help as she reached out to stop him.

'Hey, hey now. You're going to freeze to death if you carry on like this.' She admonished him but he was unresponsive, stopping because she blocked his path but saying nothing in return. The woman looked at Solace and asked angrily if he was blind.

'I'm sorry. I'm new here.' He tried to excuse his lack of action.

'How exactly does that work?' She replied indignantly, 'no ships have landed.' Then turning back to speak to the confused man she said 'You mustn't edit out the cold. You'll freeze to death. Come on, let's get inside quickly.'

Solace disconnected his thick coat and put it round the shoulders of the man, instantly feeling the biting cold. The woman nodded at him and they both led the man back towards the entrance plaza to Shelter. Once inside men in uniform came and took the stranger off their hands. The woman seemed to trust their intentions so Solace took his coat back and watched them go.

'The crew will take care of him. I have a feeling he's going to repeat his foolishness though. You can always tell the ones who're not going to make it.'

'Is it a common occurrence? You seem to know a lot about it.'

'Are you one of the people they just revived?'

'Yes, my name's Solace.'

'Renegade Potter but just call me Ren. Born on Easy Rider long after they put you to sleep. Pleased to meet you.' She thrust her wrist towards him as she said this and he, not knowing the significance, raised his own hand as if to shake hers. 'Don't you know how to bracelet bump?'

'Oh, I don't have a bracelet. Sorry,' said Solace.

'How do we keep in touch then?'

Solace, finding Renegade's company increasingly pleasant, explained that her bracelet could connect to the phone he had been given. 'But let's stick together then we won't need these devices,' he suggested hopefully.

'How long have you been awake?'

'Long enough to know that it's cold outside and you make me feel warm.'

She didn't pretend to think for long before answering with obvious pleasure, 'Well, I suppose you could do with a guide and I'm not scheduled to work today so I have plenty of time on my hands. Have you explored Shelter?'

'Is this Shelter?' he indicated the surrounding building.

'I'll take that as a "no". Let's go to Warszawa.' She took his arm and led him back into the high domed structure, smiling at him. The roof was elegant like a cluster of intricately linked soap bubbles with no obvious support.

'I'm glad we're staying inside. It stinks out there,' said Solace.

'A whole load of gross shit in the atmosphere. You wouldn't want to swallow much of it.' Her matter of fact tone softened a little as she looked up at him and continued, 'But you don't strike me as one of the lost souls who wander around naked or destroy themselves with drugs.'

'No, I just edited myself into a stupor. Or so I'm told.'

'Don't you remember it yourself?' She asked as they arrived at what looked like a coffee shop. They sat down in a booth.

'I remember my actions but since I wasn't fully aware of my condition it's not something I can remember.'

'Can we watch your memories of those last days together? I think it's good to share traumatic events.' She was already placing an order for them both on the table link, his trauma rendered ordinary.

He couldn't help but ask directly. 'Are you deliberately treating it as no big deal to make me feel better?'

She looked at him and said with obvious compassion, perhaps not for him but for some other unknown victims, 'Things got so much worse after you were put to sleep. A lot of people are dealing with tough times and you become hardened to it.'

'I'm feeling rather humble right now,' said Solace.

'Sorry to depress you. You'll be amazed how much shit people can handle though.'

'Apart from me. I fell apart.'

'Maybe your long sleep cured you of being a pussy?' she offered.

He smiled at her blunt humour. 'So, I take it from your suggestion a moment ago that you're able to show your thoughts to other people?'

'I'm no scientist but apparently it's just a development of the editing technology you remember from your time. We're just broadcasting to connected devices like the editor in our heads. Most of it isn't like a video, just a kind of gestalt or general understanding of the memory with some vivid parts unless you're very talented at editing then it can be more. They're so mutable anyway that it's kind of an art and some people broadcast better than others. Finding memories can take a while, especially if they're from a long time ago or you're only vaguely aware that you have the memory. There are gigs you can go to where people share to an entire audience. It can be pretty intense.'

'Can you broadcast to me now?'

'Yup. Catch this,' said Ren smiling at him.

'I don't think I have the tech you know. I'm getting nothing.'

'No bracelet. No modern editor. I'm surprised you're allowed shoes,' said Ren.

'I don't seem to have the ability to edit at all. Not even the old fashioned version.'

'Either somebody doesn't trust you to control your addiction or they're just cruel.'

'Looks like I have to face the full misery of this world without my comfort blanket. A man of my considerable age ought to be able to cope though,' said Solace. 'And my rejuvenated body feels fantastic so it's a fair swap.'

'Did they give you any physical upgrades?' asked Ren.

'I don't know. How can I tell?'

'I don't know without the tech in your head. Maybe you'll just have to explore your limits one day and find out,' said Ren.

'That sounds arduous. Hey, what memory did you send me?'

She laughed at him with a glint in her eye.

'That was a very dirty laugh, Ren.'

'It was a very dirty thought.'

'I've just thought of a way to explore my limits,' said Solace breaking into a dirty laugh of his own.

'Now you're getting into the Liszt spirit! Let's go to your place. I like seeing inside other people's homes.'

'I have no idea where I live,' said Solace, laughing at the absurdity of it. He thought of Karla's parting words to him earlier that day and wished he'd stayed a few minutes longer instead of walking out like there was a grand gesture to be made. 'Your place?'

'Let's go. You know, this is going to be weird, not being able to share. I'll just have to trust that you're not one of the weird ones.'

'Weird?'

'Scared to share because what's in their head is so freakish.'

'You've experienced that then?' asked Solace.

'A story for another time.'

\#

'I'm glad you found your way back here after you walked off on your own without a full induction' said Karla. 'You could easily have died on this planet.'

'I'm sorry. I was like a cool teenager ignoring his parents,' said Solace, walking into the induction room.

'Okay, well I won't ask where you've been all night then.'

'Making friends. But I've got a lot of questions for you, Karla. Why can't I edit anymore? And why don't I have one of those bracelets?'

Karla had already thought about the answers to these questions, knowing they would come. 'I had your editor upgraded but deactivated. You can get it back at a later date when you've settled into life here without resorting to the editing that mashed up your head before.' *I wish I could tell him the whole story.* He sat down and nodded blankly. She thought he still looked as if the decades might crush him one day.

'And the bracelet?'

'Well you don't really need one at the moment and all this new tech just complicates things. We'll get you one later,' said Karla.

'But don't you need one to get a car and gain entry to your home?'

'Actually your phone does both of those too,' said Karla.

'Then why does everybody have a bracelet?'

'There are a whole load of other functions that you're not going to need yet. Let me just get you adjusted to Liszt first.'

'Okay Karla, I'm in your hands.'

'First a few basics. You've already learned that you can breathe the air here. There's water here too, of course, but no significant oceans. The big problem is really the cold which is something you're just going to have to get used to. Makes you enjoy the warmth indoors more though.'

'Any indigenous life here?'

'Nothing we were able to detect beyond the micro fauna package we sent ahead years before our arrival. We've already started adapting the environment by introducing plants like grass engineered to survive here. There's a whole sequence of events planned but each stage takes time and we need to adapt as we monitor ongoing environmental changes. Right now you should be careful if you go outside of the developed areas. There are some unexpected things that can be dangerous.'

#

When he first walked into his accommodation he found it warm and pleasant. The bedroom and bathroom downstairs were designed like warm white cocoons, the sunken seating area upstairs in the living room carrying on the theme. Generous windows offered a view south over the distant factories and farms. He wondered how far he would see on a clear summer day when it eventually arrived. Not as far as the window on a spaceship. Not so far that time and space meant nothing anymore. Things he could touch, places he could walk to, people he could chase in the street, faces he could scream at.

The entrance level contained a large open room with views north over the domes of Shelter. Stairs led up to another level where a limited amount of food preparation could be done. Food production was of necessity highly efficient on Liszt. Meals were distributed free to all inhabitants through the many restaurants. To Solace, they all had an air of the student union about them. Maybe even a certain soviet bloc chic with the weather as convincing set dressing. It struck him that the entire colony was built along the lines of some utopian vision determined to impose its perfection on the climate and the people within. Visions of identical cars sliding through snow filled streets corralled by grey monolithic buildings whose narrow recessed windows hid the state machinery from view. Visions of a past before his time. Scotland and its heavy sky above housing estates and paving slabs. Which social ills was this particular utopia an answer to, he asked himself.

In the weeks that followed his revival he spent many hours sitting looking at the view and catching up on decades of brutal history and scientific advances. Ren visited every day, always excited to see him and always horny.

'I can't wait until Karla turns your tech back on. It's going to be amazing to finally share with you!'

'I get the impression you might have to wait a little longer. She avoids the topic so I don't even ask anymore,' said Solace. He wasn't sure he wanted it anyway. His addiction loomed large every time he looked out the window drinking something cold that was trying to be whisky.

'What's her problem?' asked Ren, a sullen look on her face.

'She must have her reasons. She's always cared for me and been trustworthy so I'm not going to push it.' He felt Ren's frustration and moved the topic on. 'Besides, your modern version of editing seems dangerous to me. We only used to edit our real time situation like turning down the noise but you've gone further with your excision of unwanted memories. I think that could be disastrous.'

'You try living with the trauma of sexual slavery,' said Ren.

'You did that?' Solace leaned forward as if to get up and hug her. Her bare arms looked vulnerable and cold.

'No, not me. A friend of mine.'

Solace relaxed back into his chair. 'I'm glad it wasn't you but you know I think there would be less of that sort of thing if the perpetrators couldn't erase their guilt afterwards. So much of morality is based on that guilt.'

'But it happened before we had the tech too. The sort of people who do that don't have guilt to erase,' said Ren with some passion. 'You remember I mentioned the weirdos that don't want to share?'

'Yes, when we first met.'

'When I was younger, still living on Easy Rider, I met a guy who didn't share with anybody. He said he liked figuring people out, that sharing stole the mystery and romance. It's true in a way but it gives you more than you lose. Anyway, one day instead of screwing in his cabin he took me to a part of the ship where hardly anybody went. Strange to think there was any space wasted but things fell in and out of use and there were parts nobody visited really. When we got there he asked me if I wanted to share. What he shared was like a thing rather than a person but he obviously saw himself as magnificent. I wouldn't have been surprised if he had shouted "Behold!" as he pulled the curtain aside. It was frightening enough to see inside a mind that wasn't really a whole person but it also contained the thought that he enjoyed revealing himself knowing that the other person was not going to survive the encounter, leaving him safely undiscovered. But I was more used to sharing than he was and I instinctively knew I had to act immediately before he could think my reaction.'

'What did you do?' asked Solace, unconsciously leaning forward.

'I never go anywhere without a weapon so I killed him before I had a chance to think twice,' she said in her usual blunt manner.

'I've got so many questions. Is it okay to talk about it?' asked Solace.

'Sure, I've had considerably worse experiences than that and it was decades ago. Ask away.'

'Okay. Can you explain why you say he wasn't a real person?'

'Hard to explain if you've never shared. Sharing feels like you're thinking somebody else's thoughts. You understand the difference between hearing somebody think and actually thinking their thoughts but knowing they're not your own?'

'In principle, yes, that's a clear distinction,' said Solace.

'Well the thoughts aren't just like words either. They're often complex constructs themselves and you get a flavour of the associations in the other person's mind. Imagine I let you see me thinking about the park on Easy Rider, well you might also get a sense of nostalgia and longing because I went there as a child to see trees from Earth. These other things leak out and that richness is part of why it's so wonderful.'

'That sounds absolutely amazing,' said Solace. 'Now I can't wait to share with you too. But carry on with the story, please.'

'The point was that his thoughts were less than that. I felt like they were translated from another language. Maybe you had to be him to understand them. It was only a very brief share but I kept it, not least to demonstrate my innocence, but also out of fascination.'

'Life is so hard here that I would expect a lot of damaged minds. Isn't it quite common to come across people who've done terrible things?'

'But the things will have been erased before they share with you. What you can't hide is what sort of a mind you have. That's an inadequate explanation though and you'll just have to wait to try it,' said Ren.

'If I never tried it would you think differently about me?' Ren shifted in her seat as she heard this. 'You look uncomfortable. It's okay, I'll share with you when I'm able. I want to. But does this mean you never trust somebody that won't share?'

Ren looked down at her hands as if she wasn't sure what to say. Solace followed her gaze to those neat hands and their impossibly shiny red nail varnish.

'What about privacy? Is it wrong to want privacy? What if somebody has nothing to hide, just fears being completely exposed to another person like that?'

Ren looked up. 'But it's normal. Privacy is a concept from another age.'

The answer took Solace by surprise. 'You just accidentally

reminded me that I'm a very old man. I remember times back on Earth where you could stand on top of a hill and look around over houses nestled in rolling greenery, low rise concrete schools, distant whippets looking like ants, and still feel alone with your thoughts.'

'What's a whippet?'

Solace considered her assertion that privacy was a concept from a previous age. Privacy allows you to hold opinions that you wouldn't speak publicly. Good things if you live under a tyrannical regime. On the other hand, secrets foster unhealthy stress, make it harder to be part of a community – especially if you feel shame about something. Better to get it out in public and feel free, supported. It was an interesting problem.

'Solace, you never asked how I killed him or what happened after that.'

'How did you kill him?'

'You'll find out when I share it with you one day,' she smiled.

'And what happened after that?'

'They shared my memory of the incident and concluded self-defence. They offered me some counselling but I could think of nothing worse. And that was that, no fuss.'

#

On the fringes of the city bars filled up with cold people who could never feel warm, only too hot and sick. They leaned forward into pools of light to take a sip of something medicinal: tinctures of opium, jelly tonic, olanzapine syrup, elixir of flunitrazepam.

Karla hated the bars but once in a while something dragged her back to them. She watched as a bartender, connoisseur of his own wares, shivered in the dark. He threw his long hair back then gathered it into a pony tail with sweating hands, snorted like a doped racehorse and began spinning bottles in the air with panache. The music was loud enough to be the only sound as Karla walked past the bartender through strobing lights that exaggerated her stylised movements. She watched herself in the mirror and the swing of her arse made her feel like a film star. She liked lusting eyes on her. She felt a hand take her wrist and manoeuvre her arm behind her where something thick, warm and soft arrived in her palm. She squeezed the dick once but didn't look round to identify its owner.

She sat at a sparsely populated part of the bar and waited for service. A couple of metres to her right two men sat on stools. One leaned towards the other and shouted above the music. It was just about loud enough for Karla to hear if she strained.

'Have you ever been out to Fact 10, Jethro? Did you stop anywhere near Track 6?' He turned the latest murder into a taunt.

The other man stepped down off the stool, his large form towering calmly over his inquisitor, a dismissive expression just visible on the side of his face. He appeared to say something in response then left the bar. His departure left clear space between Karla and the other man, who looked heavy and desolate and whose eyes connected with hers briefly. He took the opportunity to speak to her. It looked like he said some people just won't fit in, although she couldn't be sure. She was disgusted by him and moved away, letting the drugs take her.

Two

'It's time we made you useful again Solace. Time you joined the workforce,' Karla spoke in gentle tones.

'Hard to imagine I'll be good for anything anymore. I'm totally out of touch with everything.'

'Don't worry about that. In fact this task will bring you right up to date with life here on Liszt, which I know you've already started to understand.'

'I understand that it's a tough existence. A lot of people are traumatised by the past and have no hope for the future. But anyway, what's the job?'

Karla settled into her seat uncomfortably. 'Women disappear often on Liszt. For a planet with just one major city, a planet with fewer than a hundred thousand inhabitants, an awful lot of women go missing or are found murdered.'

'Yes, my foxy young girlfriend tells me stories about things that happen around here. I have trouble understanding it,' said Solace.

'I've noticed your relationship with Renegade Potter. It's good that you've met somebody who can help you integrate again.'

'Am I under surveillance?'

'Of course, in a friendly, big sister is looking out for you kind of way.'

'But wait, where do I fit in with the missing women?' asked Solace.

'I want you to find out who's doing it,' Karla looked directly at him.

'You want me to be a detective?' Solace had disbelief in his voice but enjoyed the idea immediately.

'In a way you're already on the job because you're looking at everything here with fresh eyes. You're not prejudiced by your own experience of our new culture and recent past.' She was leaning towards him now, hands clasped together.

'Wouldn't it be easier for me if I could access the editing and sharing tech you won't let me have? I understand your concerns over my past but really I don't feel like I did before. I have enough energy to do things.'

'We'll see about that in the future.' She adjusted herself in the chair, turning away from him a little. She was framed by the grey rectangle of light as the artificial day cast shadows that joined her to the floor. 'Right now I want you to concentrate on using your old fashioned grey matter.'

'You know this Shelter you've built reminds me of the ship. Not so much the aesthetic, although there are similarities, but the atmosphere of enclosure. The weather makes us prisoners most of the time. It's unhealthy. Your society is unhealthy. I'd say there were any number of candidates for these crimes. Where the hell do I start looking?'

'We have quite a body of evidence by now. Comprehensive files on victims, crime scenes. Forensic evidence that really should have been enough to reveal more than it has.'

'I'm assuming you've already examined everything in detail and drawn a blank?'

'Maybe not a blank but certainly no hot leads to give you. I'll give you full access to all the files and you can make of it what you will. No point in me influencing you one way or another at this point.'

'Do people have to cooperate if I want to question them?' He knew he didn't have the charm to encourage strangers to help him.

'Well, not really but I'm giving you a weapon so you can defend yourself if need be.'

'What kind of police force do we have here?' he asked. 'No authority but a weapon?'

'You're not part of our police force, Solace. I'm asking you as an individual to pursue this enquiry. I'm asking you because I trust you.'

'But you don't trust me enough to make me an official part of your police force?'

'We call them crew here. We're trying to project a feeling of togetherness and shared purpose. I think most people still feel that way,' said Karla.

'So just make me crew then? Give me some sort of authority or people won't take me seriously.'

'Look. I don't know why but I can't do it.' She sounded exasperated.

'You don't know why? What does that mean? Somebody told you not to but refused to give a reason?'

'No. I have a really strong feeling, like a directive I can't ignore, telling me not to let you have your editor yet and you can't be crew without it. Okay?' She sounded a little testy.

'Okay, sorry to push it. I trust your intentions Karla,' he sensed he ought to leave that topic. Karla had been sensitive about it from the outset for some reason. 'Shall we take a look at the files now?'

Karla swivelled her chair back towards the interior of the room where Solace sat and motioned to the wall behind him. 'Display files Misogyny.' The wall displayed a selection of folders, each with their own name – presumably that of the victim – and a date. Alongside the folders was a document entitled Investigation Summary. 'Start with the summary and work your way through. I'll be back in a couple of hours. Help yourself to refreshments while I'm gone,' she pointed at a cupboard in the corner.

Solace was shocked by the numbers. Over 130 disappearances or murders of women in the last year alone. In the same time only nine men had disappeared, none of them ever found. He wondered how so many women could disappear in a world where there are surveillance cameras and people regularly 'share' with others. If the summary was a disturbing read, the detailed files were viscerally shocking. Brutality, rape and mutilation common to them all in some fashion or other. Photos showed corpses frozen solid in the urban landscape like meat in a freezer. Three dimensional images with technical overlays of trajectories, body parts, wounds, blood splatter patterns, footprints and other forensic evidence failed to transform the scenes into an intellectual exercise.

In one file the dirty sole of a foot protruded from behind a doorway. The foreground was bright from a flash, the more distant parts dark. Solace imagined himself the killer wandering through the darkened flat stalking his victim, killing her and looking down on her corpse; the view in the photograph. It was all so real that he felt a hot nausea, resisted the primitive urge to look behind him for a witness. Then he imagined himself a detective discovering the scene, walking carefully into the room, moving closer, bending down to look at her face and know her. Pausing, locked in place for long minutes by her face until his legs complain of crouching and he has to stand. Looking around at her small, meaningless possessions. Her favourite books become just stories rather than part of a life, the keepsakes her mother brought from Earth just antiques stripped of their personal value, photos of people in long lost cities that will be forever unidentified. All of them now curiosities for collectors keen to learn as much as possible about their exciting origins.

Such an abundance of horror. Solace sat and wept with his head in his hands, totally unable to escape his imagination.

#

Solace trudged through the acrid sludge in the bare streets. The cold blue lights switched to an evening setting and their warm tones seemed to make the air thicker. Ren's living room was visible as one of many bright yellow rectangles hovering in a vague mist. He thought he saw shapes moving within and frowned to himself, hoping any guests would leave soon so that he could talk to her. All her friends seemed so similar, their opinions were identical on any topic that arose, not a single dissenting voice in the room. They had the same vocabulary, the same intonation when they spoke. When Solace commented on it to Ren one night she had laughed at him and called it friend sync, a well-known phenomenon, as if it were nothing. Solace, imagining centuries of their company, felt dread that weighed heavily on him.

Maybe it was better not to burden her with his problems. He was close enough now that his boots were tinged with the farthest reaches of light from the block entrance hall and the window was now a thin sliver of light high above.

As he approached the entrance another man came out of the misty gloom and stopped beside him.

The man motioned to the intercom, 'You first.'

Solace shrugged and pressed Ren's button. The stranger beside him adjusted his stance in a way that suggested surprise or discomfort. His face was mostly hidden but as Ren appeared on the screen he pulled back the hood of his coat and entered the camera field of view beside Solace.

Ren's face blanked for a fraction of a second, 'Solace, ask him to leave then call me back.' The screen went dark.

'Care to tell me what that was about before you go?'

The man turned to him, flesh still exposed to the cold, and stood still, challenging for more seconds than was comfortable. 'Have you ever been edited out of existence?'

Solace paused to digest this before asking, 'If she edited you out of existence then why did she not just think you were a stranger or a friend of mine?'

The man gave him a quizzical look and backed away into the mist, putting his hood up.

Solace buzzed Ren. 'He's gone. Who was he?'

'I don't know but my editor alerted me that I had previously deleted him and marked him as Avoid. Come on up.' She looked a little shaken, despite not knowing who or what she had avoided. 'And by the way, it's bad form to mention the incident from now on. There will be people in my circle that still know who that was but I just don't need to be reminded.'

#

Karla sat in her office long after she should have gone home, thinking about Solace and how she was using him. She knew he had sensitivity and that she could trust him never to cover up anything he found. She replayed a memory of him on the ship all those years ago after his editing had become a threat to his life. She had gone to his cabin to see how he was after an incident.

'Karla, I really don't need to talk about it.' But he must have known she wouldn't leave his cabin without a discussion.

'It feels like you're always angry and impatient. You never used

to be like that.' She sat to one side with her bare feet resting on his thigh.

Solace looked hurt and defensive at the accusation, as if she had piled guilt on top of his misery. He obviously didn't want to talk to her about anything but she sensed he didn't want her to give up on him either.

'Talking can't change the facts.'

'What facts, Solace?'

'We're in a Gerhard Richter landscape. You know those thick, grey skies scraped over green fields and grey box houses he painted? It might be Scotland drizzling on a grey day. I used to look at those paintings and feel nostalgia.'

'So you miss your homeland. You miss Earth. Is that it?' She was disappointed at his weakness. He had supported her on many occasions and while it was nice to be able to return the favour it was sad too.

'Miss it? No, we're in it now,' he laughed. 'It might be Cumbernauld shopping centre in the 1970s. Like a place you never particularly enjoyed and yet have nostalgia for later when you look at pictures of it. You forget how shit it was and everything looks quaint.'

'So you're saying it was shit on Earth too? I don't understand.'

'I'm saying every stage of my life so far has been unsatisfactory, mediocre, and the thought of something better always kept me going. Right now I recognise that my life is shit but I'll never look back on it from a distance and wonder how I got through it because my life will undoubtedly end on this ship before we even reach landfall. There is nothing better coming. Do you understand?'

She did understand. Then and now.

#

Ren's guests had gone, some ancient string quartet filled the room in their place, and Solace was finally able to sink into a sofa beside her. He tilted his head back and sighed, putting his arm around her shoulders. He wasn't ready to tell her about the women yet. Huge chemical snowflakes floated past outside the windows, illuminated by the glow from within against a black sky.

'You're bothered by the man at the door, I can tell.'

Surprised but accepting her misinterpretation of his pensive demeanour, Solace let a gesture confirm this false information for him.

'I don't blame you. Look. I know a little more than I told you. It's true, you can set your editor to reveal nothing but a warning but I found that just piqued my curiosity and I ended up investigating obsessively to find out who they were to me. These days, and I know that sounds as if I've done this hundreds of times, I leave an explanation for myself. I don't know his name but the man at the door was an ex of mine.'

Deciding light hearted responses about his own fate would be inappropriate, Solace asked instead if she had kept any details of the relationship.

'It's hard for people to live this long and stay together. You try tricks eventually to make things more exciting. You might decide to forget each other and start over again to recapture the honeymoon period. There are people who do it every six months. They compare it to a favourite book that can now be read again fresh.'

'In my day we couldn't even edit memories, just enhance our experiences as they happened. Anyway, isn't it hard to throw away all the years you've spent together?'

She looked at him with incredulity. 'Of course it fucking is, you idiot.' She laughed.

He felt himself blush. 'I guess that was a stupid question. I just didn't want to make any assumptions about things I know nothing about.'

'Sorry,' she snuggled against his shoulder. 'Didn't mean to make you feel shitty. You should know by now that pretty much everything here is hard and you're a pussy.'

He shrugged as if to say *but of course!*

'Every time you edit a partner out it feels worse than death because you know they're still out there missing you and you won't even feel a thing. It's best to make a mutual pact.'

'I suppose the pain goes away as soon as you forget they exist though, right? I mean it's mercifully short?' asked Solace.

'There's a vague feeling of loss. You know you're missing somebody and that's sad but you have nothing to hang the feelings on so you just gct on with life.'

'So you edited a partner out, preferably a mutual act, why does he then show up at your door?'

Ren, turning side on so she could lie back and put her legs across his knee said, 'he didn't keep his side of the pact. The note I left to myself says we edited each other out several times until I discovered that he was an evil manipulative bastard who just kept getting me to forget what a shit he was to me so he could start again. An eternal cycle of abuse that I couldn't remember.'

Solace felt an anger rising in him and had to force himself to remain seated. Ren took his hand and gave it a squeeze.

'It's nice to see you care about me but what happened before you arrived on the scene is done and forgotten so don't you worry about it or let it make you angry.'

'I was right there beside him. I could have shot him in the face and left him in the fucking street.'

'Shot? You have a gun?' Ren sat up, swung her legs to the ground and stood. 'If you have a gun you really need to control your anger. Do you have a gun?'

'She gave it to me today. I was going to tell you about it but there's some other stuff that left me feeling pretty disturbed and I wasn't sure I was able to burden you with it.'

She sat back down looking agitated but supportive. 'You'd better tell me about it now you've mentioned it. Curiosity will get the better of me every time.'

'You look nervous so let me just say first that nothing bad has happened to me, okay?'

'If I look nervous it's because I'm used to understatement when people talk about bad news.'

'Understandable.' He paused but couldn't think of anything other than a straight question, 'what do you know about the women being murdered?'

'We live in a society that not only tolerates violence against women but helps facilitate it. It's why almost all of my friends are women and I can tell you we're scared but we're also fucking angry. What does it have to do with you?'

'Karla wants me to find out who's doing it.'

Her eyes like wet glass, she took his hand and lay back. She cried energetically for a moment. 'That's so fucking exciting! Tell me the rest.'

'I can kind of see why she asked me. I'm coming at it with a different viewpoint and might notice things the crew have become inured to. Looking through the files today left me emotionally wrecked.' As he said it she squeezed his hand a little more and cried audibly before getting it back under control.

'If she's asking you then she doesn't trust the crew to resolve it. Maybe she doesn't trust her bosses either. Have you met anybody else in her office?'

'No, just her actually. And she said I couldn't be crew because I don't have an editor.'

'Everybody has an editor, not just crew, but it's interesting that not having it disqualifies you from their ranks.'

'Perhaps so that they can use shared memories as evidence if something is in dispute?'

'It's a possibility,' but Ren didn't sound convinced. 'How many files are there?'

'More than 130 this year alone,' he expected more sobbing from Ren but her face had hardened. 'Just reviewing them is horrific but what happens when I have to go to a real crime scene? And what do I know about being a detective?'

'Don't worry you have friends to help you now. Lots of them.'

'What do you mean?'

'I told you we were angry but I didn't tell you that we're getting organised too. We're trying to gather information ourselves because so little comes out from official sources. You're about to become the first man to join our organisation. And we're about to get access to those files.'

'I could certainly do with help but what do I tell Karla?'

'Nothing,' she looked incredulous. 'You're her pet project and she trusts you. She doesn't know me and my friends and she won't let us get involved.'

'She might surprise you. I feel bad at the thought of lying to her.'

'You think she's being completely honest with you? She woke you up to use you. Toughen up!'

It was true that he was being used but Karla was a good woman that had been a good friend to him. 'Okay but I'll have to tell her the full story eventually.'

'You're very loyal, I'll give you that. Right now though, tell me about the files you remember.'

#

The woman sitting opposite Solace and Ren still looked cold after her extended walk outside. She had left her bracelet behind with a friend to avoid its tracking system logging her proximity to Ren's bracelet. Liszt was far from a totalitarian state but the women took precautions on the basis that until they knew who was covering up murders it was better that they avoid becoming associated with each other. Of course without a bracelet she lost her ability to make use of the shared transport systems and had to walk instead but since the cars had internal surveillance they had to be avoided anyway.

'First let's look for any statistical analysis they've done on the files. See if there's any kind of pattern they're working on.'

'If the investigations were sloppy then the raw data for statistical analysis is compromised. We need to go back to basics.'

'Karla cares about this. She would only trust data she could verify. See if we can get her take on the analysis and in the meantime let's assess their investigations.'

'Let's do some work on the most recent murder. Evidence will be fresher for that one. We need that file Solace.'

'What if your investigations get back to the crew and they realise I'm passing information?'

'One case isn't enough to give you away. And we'll be careful. Prepare a cover story in case our investigation is noticed.'

'The one out at Fact 10, Track 6 is the most recent. I'll get the file.'

'Doesn't that archaic phone Karla gave you take pictures?'

'Yes. Why?'

'To bring copies of the file, dummy. Have you never seen the old spy films?'

'Why don't I just ask her how I can access the files from other locations? How am I supposed to work without the files? And she's not the enemy.'

Three

Karla lay in a hot, deep bath with steam rising around her. It occurred to her that back on Earth baths had come in all different shapes and sizes but here on Liszt the spacious regulation size bath was better than them all. Some designer had obviously realised from the outset that the cold climate made soaking in a bath more important than ever.

She watched the footage of Solace meeting Ren and her friend to discuss the investigation. What an amazing bonus it had been that Solace had met a woman who was part of a group that could become Karla's own unwitting task force. She desperately wanted to tell Solace that she knew about and fully approved of his new friends but she had no idea who might be surveilling her so she kept quiet for now. She wondered if Solace realised he was in love with Ren. If he didn't reject the feelings then perhaps it would help him value the future again. A century ago Karla and Solace had loved each other as they sat looking out of a window on space. Thinking about her long life and the past made her uncomfortable to the point of anxiety but she was long past caring about the artificiality of an edited life and quelled her discomfort with a thought.

The door was open so that she could hear the ancient Gregorian chants she had been enjoying earlier in the living room. There were speakers in every room but sometimes she preferred to hear the music from another room. When she was a child classical music would emanate from her father's domain, the living room, and permeate the whole house.

All the sounds changed as she lowered her ears under the water, keeping her head level to avoid letting the water flood in deeper. As she closed her eyes she heard a familiar tone from her bracelet ping through the bathwater like a submarine sonar. Sitting up, she projected the image from her bracelet onto the wall in front of her.

'We've caught one!' said the excited face that filled her wall.

'What?' she asked before realising that her colleague Naz could only be referring to one thing, 'In the act?'

'Literally in the act. Caught him fucking the still warm corpse, covered in blood and guts.'

Karla screwed up her face at the thought of it. 'Please tell me you incapacitated him before he could edit?'

'Caught totally unaware and zapped from behind by drone. He won't even know we've caught him until he wakes up.'

Karla stepped out of the bath, 'Wait until I get there.'

She heard him apologise for interrupting her bath as she ended the call.

#

Solace sat alone in Warszawa drinking some sort of pale tea from a small transparent cup. It wasn't clear to him what he wanted to think about so he sat and waited. He watched the everyday movement of people through the street beside the café. Without much work for human hands there was plenty of time to contemplate a future too short to reach beyond this pioneer age. *It's not much different from our time on the ship. A common goal. No need for money, wealth or competition for resources. So much free time but people do nothing with it because they feel hopeless. Some of these people have the look of weary boxers out on their feet. Fatigue. They don't see it though. They edit it out like I used to do but it's still there. Lethargy, depression, no enthusiasm for the future.*

He stood up, remaining by his table. After a while his vertical form attracted a couple of nosy glances but most people ignored him. He stood in the middle of the street and watched people pass by oblivious but without bumping into him. *Is their reality the same as mine? Is this an empty street to them?* He remembered the case of some poor guy he heard about on Easy Rider, he believed he was dead after he survived a suicide attempt. The brain has long been constructing realities based on beliefs.

He meandered through the streets. They were deliberately narrow in this area to recreate the mood of a medieval city. Moving much more slowly than other people he felt like a rock in river. He paid more attention than usual to the details around him. The streets here were paved with hard ceramic tiles laid in attractive geometric patterns, the entrances to restaurants and cafes blended the tiles into their own style seamlessly. Time had been spent on form as well as function here just like it had on the ship.

He took a circuitous route towards Karla's office. He hadn't really made an effort to connect with her since she had awakened him and he felt guilty about it. Walking through the lonely crowds, he wondered if she had become one of them. He wanted to talk to her about the way people were living now but he didn't want her to think he was slipping back into his previous state of hopelessness. Part of him didn't want to risk being taken off this project she'd given him and knowing this made him feel more guilt as if he was using her. This manipulative behaviour, withholding information to achieve a certain outcome, was not something he could continue.

Upon arriving at the office he found it empty and made himself at home. After a brief discussion with the computer it granted him remote access to the files, a permission that Karla had already set. Feeling a little like an intruder in her office, he left to investigate the files elsewhere. He would call Ren on the way and she could arrange for one of her secret society friends to come along and pore over the data with them.

Solace journeyed back through the indoor streets towards the biting cold exterior. He hated the cold but found Liszt beautiful, both as a striking urban environment and as a tragic romantic setting. He invented stories for the people he saw.

In parts of Shelter there were play houses where sex parties and nude bathing went on all day and night. He had seen these first hand on one of Ren's guided tours. He wondered, as the number of bodies in the pool that evening was already reduced in number from the height of the party, if there would be one last man gently floating in the cum with steam rising from his chest, his eyes opening finally to discover he's alone. Solace saw hedonistic escapism as something to be enjoyed for a time but imagined the more thoughtful would drift away from it after a while, looking back with a vague loneliness. Ren hadn't asked him to stop and sample the delights on their tour.

Out in the burbs a small group of women made their way home. The wind smelled of ammonia and flattened their coats against their chests. It was hard to be heard over the wind so they didn't speak much as they walked. One of them would be dreaming of training to become a nurse so that she could leave behind the grinding mental assault of feeling useless. She would be dead in a few days and her friends would raise a glass to her memory but fear to talk of it openly, not knowing who might be listening or who might be next. They had their own dreams that hadn't quite been beaten or that Solace hadn't yet imagined for them. Each street lamp dropped a cone of light on the slush.

These sentimental imaginings feed my despair. If I could stop it I'd probably be happier. Think less and do more.

Walking figures didn't travel as far as the factories – they were spaces where people never went in person. The fear of dangerous processes, chemicals that might burn, corrode or poison humans kept them at bay. They were voids that you drove through on your way to the farms or on your way home to the residential areas from the farms. Since so few people worked in the farms that meant that most parts of the factories never saw a human from one year to the next. Drones patrolled and diligent algorithms searched their feeds for problems or anomalies. Things were refined, transformed and made all day every day for the furtherance of the colony. Their dramatic appearance was an important part of their function.

The gardeners worked the farthest out, if you excluded the explorers who insisted that human observation was still a useful way to investigate other places on the planet. The gardeners didn't get their hands dirty as the fully automated factory farms had no need for human intervention. They were just caretakers rather than gardeners really although even when things broke down it would be robots that effected repairs. Sometimes they would stop to smell the plants or stroke a leaf in passing, which was their true reason for choosing the job.

Solace arrived at Ren's flat just after her friend Dascha. They all sat in the living room projecting the murder at Track 6 onto the wall. They had planned to talk to the victim's friends, look where she travelled and figure out how she got there, who she might have met. The files showed this work already complete with interviews and testimonies. The crew had done a thorough job not just with friends and acquaintances but strangers passing through the district where she lived or near the crime scene. There was no lack of effort, which surprised the women.

Karla's notes detailed her thoughts on location tracking. The victim's bracelet was left in the hallway of her residential block. That may have been planned. Taking a bracelet to a restricted area like a factory would have created automatic alerts for crew to investigate or at least the dispatch of a drone. Leaving her bracelet out in the street, static, would have created an automatic hypothermia risk alert to the bracelet and any crew in the area. Leaving her bracelet in public places like cafes would have been difficult because cameras would surely show the murderer himself leaving it there. Inside her own hallway was the safest place to avoid causing an alert.

The bracelet began its long wait late in the evening. There had been very few other bracelets nearby at the time and none of them stopped moving in her vicinity, suggesting that the murderer hadn't been wearing one either. Did he walk there? Karla's notes wondered. Was he alone? The scene of the crime is more than a kilometre from her residence. It seems likely that (a) he had help to convey the victim that far without being noticed or (b) the victim was known to the killer and went with him willingly or (c) the victim was drugged into compliance.

Having read much of the file in silence they turned to one another to discuss it, subdued.

'There's more work in there than I expected,' said Dascha. 'There are no obvious gaps we can investigate and no work that seems badly executed first time round.'

'Let's have a look at the detailed forensics.'

Footage from the drone that discovered the corpse filled the wall, giving them a larger than life view. Drifting down towards the ground, so close in to her skin that it had the appearance of a vast icy landscape shot from above. Solace imagined himself to be the killer inspecting his victim as the camera drifted round further to view her genitals frosting over next to the steaming wound of an amputated leg.

'I'm not sure how much we're learning from this footage,' said Solace as an invitation to stop it.

Dascha looked over at him, 'we have to be thorough. Look away if you've no stomach for it.'

'I sat through it once before. I'm telling you it does nothing but disturb the viewer.'

'I'm not disturbed, just fucking angry at the men that do these things.'

'Did you know that when people are editing out their emotions they have a particular facial expression?'

Dascha went a little red at the suggestion but said nothing in reply.

'Okay sorry but these are my files and I'm telling you this gore isn't helping anything. Look at the traffic nearby at the time of the incident. You would expect the crew to have interviewed anybody passing her building near that time but there are no vehicles there for ten minutes either side of the incident.' He pulled up a map view of the streets with blinking dots showing vehicles moving along the roads. 'Five minutes before all the cars start turning off onto other streets. Isn't that a little odd? The circuitous routes can't possibly be the most efficient route to their destinations. What does this suggest to you?'

'The road was blocked?'

'No, that would have been a significant operation that attracted attention. The crew would have heard about it and investigated.'

'What then?'

'The cars did drive past and somebody might have seen something so the data was altered. That way none of the drivers would be questioned as potential witnesses.'

'Nobody can hack the systems. There are no recorded incidents of it ever happening. It's guarded by layers of semi-sentient systems monitoring each other. The programs are audited regularly by machine and human.'

'She's right,' said Ren. 'It's inconceivable. There hasn't been a single hacking incident since we began our journey from Earth.'

'Even so we have nothing to lose by interviewing the people in the cars that made slightly odd detours during that time. Detours that meant the crew didn't bother to interview them as potential witnesses to the snatching of our victim from her hallway.'

'If there's any truth in this people will freak.' Dascha leaned back, her arms out to either side across the top of the sofa. 'But give me the driver's details and I'll get some of the women to talk to the drivers. We'll be subtle and maybe we can share with them.'

'That would be incredibly useful, thank you,' said Solace. Her face told him he was patronising or annoying her in some way but he left it there.

Four

Leaving the women to carry out their own investigation, Solace had come to one of the many bars. It was still relatively early in the day and patrons were thin on the ground. The artificial daylight of Shelter streamed through the still air, surprisingly bright. It reminded Solace of the winter light shining through the windows of a restaurant in the shadow of the Forth Rail Bridge back on Earth.

In a booth nearby the light struck craggy angles on the faces of two in sporadic conversation. Solace watched them discretely, feeling entitled to do so in his new role as investigator. The one called Jethro turned his full attention now on the other, Joao. He faced him and paused, looking like a young Joe Dallesandro. Solace watched the air between them charge with expectation and glinting dust like a cloud of asteroids seen from afar.

'Have you ever ventured beyond the farms on foot? Not just at the edge of the farm but far enough that you can't see the factory towers anymore.' Jethro spoke slowly and quietly but the bar was quiet and Solace could hear clearly.

'The train stopped in the middle of nowhere once. We got out and walked around a little. There was nothing to see,' said Joao.

'I bet you didn't stray far from the tracks,' Jethro kept his gaze fixed on Joao, 'but that's not the point. I'm not just interested in the wilderness itself. This is about people.'

'Other people go out past the farms on foot? Why? There's nothing there.'

'There's nothing here either.' And he laughed at his own joke.

He's verging on psychotic, thought Solace. 'We're the in between people. We never saw the beautiful Earth and we won't live long enough to see Liszt blossom. There's nowhere else we can go, nothing else we can do. This shit is all we have.' He raised his glass to his lips, the light catching the blonde hairs on his thick forearm.

Joao appeared momentarily confused. 'I suppose that's true but how can you miss what you never had?'

Jethro started to stand up but stopped himself and carried on talking. 'A baby born in a vacuum would miss oxygen. This is not our natural habitat. It fails to satisfy our basic human needs. Anyway, we've all seen the archives.'

'And you think this is why somebody is killing those women?'

'There are thousands of men on Liszt who feel there's nothing to live for, that they have no future and no power. Nothing will ever satisfy them. I'm surprised there aren't more suicides than murders.'

'People say you trawl the burbs every chance you get.'

Jethro stood up, sighed and turned to leave without another word. Solace waited a few seconds then followed him out of the bar. Somebody had just put a song on the jukebox.

'Wait!' called Solace.

Jethro stopped and turned around, 'What?'

'I overheard your conversation in the bar.'

'Then you're a nosy bastard,' said Jethro but he didn't walk away.

'You're the first person I've heard vocalise what I've been thinking and feeling about life here,' said Solace. Jethro said nothing in return but let his gaze drift across Solace's face which Solace experienced as a wave of compassion. Jethro stepped forward and hugged him.

'Don't you share?' asked Jethro after a moment.

'I can't. Long story.'

'I've seen the people that seep in and out of the editing support groups, dude. No need for a story.'

'I heard your friend say you like to trawl the burbs.'

Jethro returned his gaze. 'Want to come for a drive?'

A rugged car arrived for them at the bottom of the tunnel, dark liquid already dripping from its underside.

Jethro drove up the ramp and onto one of the wide streets that radiated from the sheltered zone towards the factories and farms. Ahead, streets branched off at regular intervals into the towering burbs. In the rear view, Shelter was a collection of brightly lit blisters filled with tall trees.

The streets, never busy, were empty now and the car sent a spray of slush metres into the air on either side as it picked up speed. To the left and right, all the streets looked the same and nothing moved. Domestic towers varied in height and aspect, room layouts were fluid, but the lives within were standard.

The sound of the road filled the cabin. The dense atmosphere transmitted the sound through echoing chasms between the factory towers. The lights, pipes and occasional flames of industrial processes spoke of transformation. The fog was thick and the vast ring of lights became a spectral glow in the distance with dark jutting angles protruding from it closer to the road. After some time the factories weren't there anymore but the road continued straight ahead. Solace looked across at the many facets of Jethro reflected in curved windows with lights moving and glistening on the gleaming black interior. His hands on the wheel and his gaze straight ahead. Bodies started to smell like sex in the warm space. Solace didn't care where they went so long as the journey continued.

Orderly curving rows of greenhouses and interlocking tunnels disappeared into the misty distance on both sides. The car sped through this deep ring of industrial farming while occasional shadows moved alone between the sheltered plants. Glasshouses gave way to flat cultivated fields in all directions. The fog was thinner here and black sky arced down to the horizon.

Finally the last trace of habitation was the road itself and Jethro drove on faster until the car seemed to be floating across the ground.

#

'At last!' said Naz. 'Can we finally wake this bastard up?'

'Calm down, I haven't even taken my coat off,' said Karla as she moved about the office preparing for a moment they had all waited years to experience. 'I take it you weren't too excited to go through prep according to procedure?'

'He's boxed and hooked up so we have full control of his editor. We can wake him up anytime you like. We'll see his editing commands on the screen in text but it'll only take him seconds to realise he's got no control.'

'Okay I read his file in the car on the way over. Unless I'm imagining something, this is the most boring file we have on anybody. Deek Brown. He's done literally nothing of note in his entire life to date. He's like a rough sketch of a person waiting to be fleshed out later.'

'If you've got dark secrets the last thing you want is to attract attention. Old Deek just kept his head down.'

'I know but he's in his sixties. It's hard to be so disciplined for that long. Still, if we've got nothing then we've got nothing. I take it the rest of the team are in the observation lounge?'

'It's a full house for this one.' He looked behind and untinted the window so a wall of faces were visible for a second before he flicked the switch back again.

'Let's get started,' said Karla. 'Dark the box. We'll wake him up with zero indication of where he is.'

'Box is dark. Waking him now.'

Inside the box there was no light or sound to betray the location. Hopefully Deek would wake up thinking he was in bed at home.

Delete all appeared on the screen.

'That was quick!'

Delete all.

'It must have been his first thought.'

Delete last 24 hours.

'Who wakes up and instantly commits virtual suicide? There's no way he could have known he was captured. No way he could have known he was in our box.'

Lock sharing.

'Too late, suicidal Deek.'

Record all.

'I've never seen anything like this guy. Let's stand his box up and get a light on him.'

Naz obeyed Karla's instructions and the box slid upright in front of them, its walls transparent to them now and light shining on Deek who remained static in the box. Without apparent sign of tension he cast his gaze around the room and at Karla and Naz directly.

'Let him hear us,' she motioned to Naz who complied, 'Deek. We're very pleased to finally meet you.'

Deek made no reply.

'You won't remember because we rendered you unconscious whilst you were raping the corpse but you should know we have everything we need already. This is just your opportunity to cooperate with our process. We don't need your cooperation, as you know, but we might be kinder to you if we have it.' She nodded and Naz cut the feed. The box went dark again. 'Let him stew while we have a cup of tea. I doubt he'll say anything before we start poking around in his head but he deserves to sweat a little anyway.'

'He doesn't look like he's sweating. He was prepared to delete himself from the outset too. Seems to me that he's done things so awful that he knows he'll never be free. It's a choice between incarceration or execution and he'd rather choose his own moment.'

'You're right. He doesn't look bothered. His very first waking thought was to delete his own personality. Most people have that command buried deep in a series safeguards and confirmations. He has it as a root command.'

'So his finger is always on the trigger?'

'Maybe. I'm not sure yet but there's something odd going on. Let's bring the lights up again then we'll start digging.'

The box lit up and Deek was revealed in the same position as before.

'Last chance Deek. Talk or be our entertainment for the next few days as we laugh at your most intimate moments.' She waited a second or two knowing there would be no response. 'Okay Naz let's share whatever he's got. Might as well make it truly public,' she made a sweeping gesture towards the observation lounge as Naz flicked the switch to make them visible and audible. A cheer went up.

Autoshare on request appeared on the screen, briefly attracting Deek's attention.

'Let's start a few hours ago. Do you remember what you were doing then Deek?' She didn't need to ask as his memories were available now to them all. She didn't want to be the first to delve into his sickness. In fact she didn't want to go in there at all. 'Dark the box Naz. He doesn't need to see or hear us anymore.' She didn't want him to see discomfort on her face as she shared his memories.

The cheering was long gone now. Everybody was immersed in the last memories. Brief bursts, skipping backwards to locate the beginning of the crime. He was picking her up off the ground to take her deeper into the factory. Naz skipped back a little further in time but there was nothing there. He went forward at normal speed until once again he arrived at the point where Deek had picked her up off the ground. Before that there was absolutely nothing.

'No memories before he found her unconscious by the road.' Naz turned to Karla as he stated the obvious.

'He must have wiped himself clean just prior to that point. Covering his tracks as he went along. Perhaps protecting an accomplice. That's beyond cautious. Go further back. Let's find his first memory before that point.'

Naz skipped back further. 'Nothing for a week,' he kept going. 'Nothing for a month. Removing time constraints… nothing fresh at all. The man's got a totally blank period that lasts years. No wonder he was prepared to delete the few memories he had.'

'How far back does it go?'

'Far enough that I can't be precise. It must be decades. This kind of examination is beyond my abilities.'

'I think we're going to need a technical and forensic analysis.' Karla slumped in her chair, deflated by this new complexity and delay.

Hoping she looked calm, Karla thought about the ramifications. A man so willing to wipe his own memories was a frightening prospect. For most people a total wipe was the equivalent of death. Many people edited out painful sections of their lives but not Karla. She held tight to the integrity of her memory. As soon as you leave gaps you make yourself vulnerable to deceptive people. Strange that Solace, who she trusted above almost anybody else she'd ever met, relied upon his human baseline standard memory. A notoriously fallible memory prone to invention and error that editing technology had almost replaced in recent decades. She urgently needed to know what Deek had done to his editor and how he had achieved it.

Two editing technicians entered the room. Karla would have struggled to remember their names as she had little to do with them and they tended to keep low under the radar but her tech presented the information anyway. 'Dayron and Heidi. My two best techs.'

She received a slightly embarrassed smile from Dayron before he looked at her tits then opened up his kit on the desk. Heidi looked impatient. Maybe she had more interesting things to do back in the lab. 'Is there a specific issue you want us to address?'

'Yes but I'd rather get you to run a complete diagnostic and tell me what you find.'

'Okay but that's going to take a few hours.'

'Naz, stay with them. Call me when you're ready.'

#

'Where are you Solace?'

'Just lying on the couch thinking.' *And before that I was setting foot on the substance of this alien planet for the first time. My flesh on the freezing surface for a few seconds.* 'Where are you?'

'Working. We've caught one of the killers in action.'

Solace sat up on the couch, surprised but suddenly uncertain, 'Why don't you sound more excited about it?'

'Almost all of his memories are already gone. He's virtually a blank except for the murder itself.'

'Shit, he wiped before you put him under?'

'No, he was already like that. He seems to have deleted his entire life as a mere precaution.'

'That doesn't make sense,' he was up from the couch and walking around to stimulate his thinking. 'You know, you people have edited out so much that your experience is no longer just an enhanced version of events but your own interpretation. Memories were always ephemeral and prone to confabulation but you've elevated that to an art. You sit in the same room together but some of you are in different worlds. What you see and hear is totally corrupted until it's just what you want to be there. You craft your experiences and your memories like art.' He spoke with enthusiasm and speed.

'You think we haven't thought about that? Can we get back to my killer please?' Karla sounded flat with disappointment and didn't seem interested in Solace's realisations.

41

'Public sharing drives narcissism which leads to perfectionism in the creation of memories for sharing. Your achievements become instant dramatised documentaries. I bet crimes are treasured and collected too! I bet your criminals have their own secret clubs for sharing. There's no way he deletes all his kills.'

'Creeps like this always end up editing. Of course they want to keep and treasure their memories of the crimes but they also want to do it again. They make heavy edits then regret it. We've all done it on a lesser scale. Something bad happens and you delete it. Reset your life as far as you can but make a hell of a mess in the process.'

'Are you speaking from experience?' Solace felt an opportunity to bond with Karla again by exploring what sounded like a personal regret. 'Have you regretted deleting something?'

'Not lately. But the point is it's like cheating at life. There's no satisfaction if there's no risk. For criminals there's a risk in keeping the memories but a desire not to lose them. The bigger the crime the bigger the risk.'

She was all business so he stayed on topic. 'Even if you delete it can you be sure nobody else knows? Imagine you're a crook and you delete a crime – how far do you go? Do you, is it even possible, to delete not just the crime but also your motive for the crime?'

'I've investigated deeper on cases where suspects have no memory of the night in question. There are always clues in your memory that a good detective can piece together later. It's why criminals often delete much more than they really want to. Too many crimes and they lose their identity eventually. It's a kind of death.'

'So where does this leave us? Would he delete his memories or not? Either he leaves clues and gets caught out eventually or he wipes more than he wants to. I think those crimes mean too much to be deleted.'

'We're in agreement,' said Karla. 'Which leaves an uncomfortable conclusion.'

'Somebody else wiped him.'

'And that's not supposed to be possible. I've got technicians working on his editor now to see what they can find. I'm shitting myself.'

'Shall I come in?'

'No, I haven't really told any of the guys about you.'

'Why not?'

'I'm not sure. Whenever I think about it a have a strong urge to keep quiet.'

#

'Where did you get this guy?' asked Heidi.

'Get him? He's not an artefact, he's a person.'

'Interesting that you took it that way,' Heidi cocked her head. 'Must have been something in the way I said it that gave away the subtext. Anyway he kind of is an artefact.'

'How so?' said Karla.

'First, his editor is attached to a receiver unit that can be used as a controller rather than just for sharing, unlike the standard units we have. Second, its commands have been modified, as you noticed earlier on the screen, so the defaults are really strange. Third, there's a set of commands and algorithms programmed for certain behaviour patterns inside the controller unit. In other words, he's a remote controlled body that can be wiped at any time and still function on the basic protocols in his tech. He's not a person anymore by any reasonable standard.'

Karla felt dazed and disconnected. She heard Naz, standing behind her, ask if he was an automaton or if he had free will.

'I'm not sure,' said Dayron. 'Until now I was aware that it was possible to do this with editors. Obviously it wasn't designed with this purpose in mind and there are safeguards against its misuse. Difficult to imagine what it must be like to be on the receiving end but I suppose it might feel like you have free will even though you don't. I mean as long as you don't know the source of the instructions you could imagine them to be your own I suppose. We need to do a lot more work on this.'

'So you're telling me the guy we caught was himself a victim?' asked Karla, returning to the moment.

'Unless he volunteered for the installation of the device knowing that he would later commit crimes.'

'And you're not sure if he was acting of his own volition when he committed the crime?'

'We're really not sure how this stuff works so no, we can't tell. It's not impossible that we might figure it out though.'

'You don't make it sound likely,' said Karla, 'but we need to know. We need to know if he's a criminal or a victim or both. And we need to know who did this to him.'

'We'll find out what we can but I can't promise anything,' said Heidi, matter of fact.

'Naz, let's leave them to it. We need to brief the team.'

The observation lounge was full of nervous faces.

'All ideas are welcome but for now there are some burning questions,' began Karla. 'I'm considering the possibility that Deek Brown is just a tool used by others to collect memories of crimes to be enjoyed through sharing. Yvonne and Yost, look for any information on criminals sharing their crimes, maybe as part of some secret club. Naz, you and me will work with Dayron and Heidi to try and identify who might have been responsible for creating that Frankenstein next door. Yello, Massassi, Reuben and Natsuki, I need you to revisit all the other murders with this information in mind. There might be angles you wouldn't have considered first time around. The rest of you will be doing the spadework.' There were a few groans from the floor. 'We'll meet once a day to debrief. I promise you all this is the most important case you'll ever work.' She let that sink in for a moment. 'No loose lips, bar room chatter or overshare in the heat of passion. The ramifications could change our world so keep it locked down.'

Five

Solace and Ren sweated side by side as the virtual summertime forest scattered light through branches. Underfoot the earth felt bouncy and hollow as they ran along one of the trails. Hovering in the trees in front of them faint white text showed the time they were ahead of their last run. If they turned to look they would see themselves behind, oblivious to the new them.

'We don't spend enough time in places like this,' said Solace, finding the pace easy.

'Wouldn't want to remind myself too often how nice it is on the planet we left behind. Lots of people have started creating their own scapes of Liszt as it might look in the future.'

The gradual adaptation of Liszt to terrestrial life preferences was by no means precise. Evolution would intervene at every stage and the interactions between the micro fauna introduced and those native to Liszt were not really knowable in advance, at least not in the long term.

'Are those the ones with black trees, blue grass and purple lakes?'

'You've seen them then?'

'They're like an attempt to create a new aesthetic. I appreciate the principle of making us love what we have, very clever. Very shit

45

though.' Ren made no reply but her face formed the shape of disapproval. Solace knew she would not be rising to his bait and felt a little guilty. 'I mean they look like a chemical world and I'd rather hold out for an Earth-like environment.'

'So do you want to know some news or just continue trying to belittle our attempts to make the best of our situation?'

'I'm sorry. What news, my feisty little runner?'

Ren smacked his arse as they ran. 'You were right about the vehicles. And there was a guy who saw something he considered pretty unremarkable at the time. A big man supporting a woman on their way to the car. He said she was off her face on drugs and he wasn't much better.'

'Big?'

'Tall rather than bulky.'

'Our boy is short but very powerfully built.'

'Well that answers that. Any other news?'

'Not yet. Keep you posted.'

'Let's push on, we're only a few seconds ahead of our last run.'

#

Solace had told the women about the captured killer but hadn't gone into any detail. Feelings of betrayal had stopped him from sharing information about the editing technology or the ramifications for people on Liszt. He called Karla and found that she was at home rather than the office, for once. She invited him round and he accepted.

He checked his phone map to see how far it was. Ren said the default maps in bracelets made you feel a sense of achievement as you approached your destination. That is, if you had paired your bracelet with your editor. Solace wondered what the most popular emotion choices were: relief, happiness, erotic arousal. Maybe there was a random setting too. He arrived at his destination feeling excited, by purely natural means, and pressed Karla's buzzer.

'Yvonne and Yost came by once and made me try this cinnamon toast. I never had it back on Earth and now I have a synthetic version but I promise you it's delicious. Do you want to try some?'

Solace nodded. 'I'll give it a go.' He sat on a stool while Karla started making the toast. 'Listen, I haven't been entirely honest with you, Karla.' She waited for more, making toast and not looking him in the eye so he carried on. 'I let Ren and some friends of hers see some of your files. I also told them you caught Deek. They want to help. They told me not to tell you in case you were under surveillance. I told them you would be trying your best, no matter what. I'm really sorry I didn't come to you immediately.'

'Why did you decide to tell me now?'

'I've got new information from them but I didn't tell them about the editing tech anomalies. That's when I realised I trusted you more than Ren.' He had only just come to accept that fact and found it odd to say out loud.

'I knew about the women. It's okay. They mean well and they might even be useful to us.'

Solace breathed a sigh of relief. 'They've already been useful. They found a witness to the abduction and his description confirms that it wasn't Deek. And also that the recorded route of their vehicle was inaccurate, or deliberately altered.'

Karla put a plate of cinnamon toast on the counter. 'The women were right to be cautious then. I'm not sure where we go from here.'

'You know it's the first time I've been in your flat? I felt excited as I came here today.'

'Excited?' Karla tilted her head and smiled.

'I don't know why, exactly.'

'Do you remember our time together? It's a century ago for me but only a handful of years ago for you.'

'Of course I remember. I'm sorry I was badly behaved. How about you, is it lost in another life? I feel like a living fossil.'

'You're not a lost relic in my mind. Memories are made and remade all the time as you use them. The old fashioned ones anyway. You were a memory that I revisited a lot over the years. By the time editors could hold memories locked in amber forever my memories of you were probably already fictions.' She laughed, 'I turned you into a legend.'

Solace wasn't sure how to react. He wondered how life would be if he had the ability to directly access and understand his emotions. He wondered if he would always know what to do. 'I suddenly feel guilty about being here.'

'The guilt isn't about being here, it's because you liked what I just said and you feel emotionally attached to me. You're thinking about Ren.'

'Yes,' he realised she was right. Other people always saw his emotions better than he could. 'I feel very protective of her. She's been through a lot and we've bonded together. She helped me look up some people I once knew. What a fucking disaster. Half of them had died before the anti-senescence treatments became so effective. Suicide too. I was astonished by how many of my friends killed themselves. I went to meet a couple of the survivors but they were strangers to me. You're the only link to my past Karla.'

'I thought about how tough it would be for you to adjust. I didn't give it much thought, just a little guilty twinge before I woke you up. I've been through a lot too. A lot of it before Ren was born. I'm pushing two centuries Solace. We're like vampires stalking the night, growing bored with each other, forgetting what it was like to play in the sun. People do horrible things under stress and I've been cleaning it up for decades.'

'Living and working in the darker side of human nature. But now there's a semblance of happiness, even if it's edited into existence, isn't it getting easier?'

'Now I don't know what's real. I don't know if my thoughts are my own.'

'You know they used to ask that on psych evaluations?' Solace regretted his attempt at humour as soon as it left his mouth. Karla ignored it.

'My memories of you predate my current concerns. When I think of you I'm taken back to a whole world that doesn't exist without you.'

'When we first met it was still thrilling to stand in the park and look out at the stars, wondering what landfall would bring. I knew we might end up with an inhospitable world, I knew we might go mad with boredom on the way here, but I never imagined the reality of it.'

'That was a time before the real trouble began. We were riding a wave of optimism like the 1950s. Maybe if we talk about it we can spread the optimism like some sort of social contagion.' She casually brushed the back of her hand against his.

'Your cinnamon toast is delicious,' said Solace, not knowing where to take the conversation next. Hairs on his arm stood up. He paid attention to the details of Karla's body: a mole on her arm, the curve of a nostril, the flecks of green in her grey eyes. He didn't want to talk now.

Karla, sitting on the stool with knees raised to her elbows, rested her chin on her fists. 'Let's get your women to do something useful. Let them look for signs of women being abused in other ways. Maybe they know somebody who has memory blanks they can't explain. Women who felt compelled to behave in a way they can't understand. The sort of thing you might mention to a friend in passing because it was nagging at you.'

'You think everybody can be controlled by their editor? I thought the tech in Deek's head was an anomaly?'

'His editor had some algorithms we don't understand yet and was controllable from a distant device he had no control over. Standard editors can be paired with our bracelets to bring in new data that supplements certain limited functions like location maps, habitat information, phone or video calls. The owner of the editor and the bracelet has total control over that pairing, can cut it at any time. I'm just questioning the truth of that belief.'

'Have you any reason to believe people are being tampered with?' Solace was already thinking back to the days on Earth when governments and powerful people controlled the world through misdirection and manipulation. On Easy Rider and now on Liszt every adult had the right to vote on any decision that needed to be made. All decisions were a matter of public record. 'I'm not sure what the motivation would be.'

Karla took his hand in both of hers, 'Solace, always so innocent.' She smiled warmly at him. 'Sometimes people are cunts.'

'I assume you'll get your techs to work on that premise too then? See if there's some way it could happen.'

'Yes. In the meantime I've unpaired my bracelet.'

'You must be feeling vulnerable,' he could see her straining to contain some emotion or other. He thought it might be sadness or maybe fear. He stepped down from his stool, encouraging Karla to do the same by putting his hands on her shoulders and pulling her towards him gently. In an awkward movement he pulled her into a hug, feeling all the time that she might not want to be hugged by him.

'I'm sorry, this feels sexual,' she said as she released him.

Solace, felt embarrassment and disappointment. 'When I asked for my editor to be activated you said you had a strong feeling you couldn't ignore that told you not to do it.'

'Yes.' Her body language lacked any confidence.

'Do you think you could be one of the women we're looking for? Did you feel compelled?'

'Well, going against it would have made me angry.'

'But if somebody was controlling people through editors they would want me to have the tech switched on, right?'

'Yes. I wondered if I had developed a mental illness, that I had another personality telling me what to do. If you don't know where your thoughts come from it's easy to feel that way.'

'What if you created the thought then deliberately forgot the reasons behind it?' it was the simplest explanation.

'To hide my knowledge from somebody that could see inside my head without permission…'

'Wait, don't you let people control your thoughts through sharing their experience?'

'No, that's just like playing a tape. It doesn't give control access, just data access to your internal tape player. But you might be on to something with the deliberate forgetting. Maybe I thought I would be questioned by crew about something. We're the only ones with the tech to do it.' Solace was surprised by the sudden and dramatic change in her mood. She seemed to have instantly forgotten about her fears.

\#

Feeling strangely comfortable in the car with Jethro, Solace sank back and looked out the window. He enjoyed ceding control. It was a luxury like no other.

Although Jethro assured him they were on a different road to last time the sights were very much the same. The layout of the colony was circular so whatever spoke you drove out on, you went through the same zones. The windows were a cinema of reflected lights and distant factories. He didn't want to ruin the atmosphere with talk but wondered if Jethro felt as he did.

'Have you ever brought somebody with you before?'

Without engaging autodrive, Jethro turned to look at Solace. 'Brought? No, but people are the reason I come out here.'

'We were alone last time.'

'If you come often enough you eventually meet other people' His tone was factual and implied that nothing further needed to be said.

'You go there to meet people?'

Jethro sighed heavily and turned round once more, 'I know you don't edit but if you like I can share something with you just once and you'll get it. It's so much quicker than explaining everything in verbals.'

'I'm physically incapable. My editor is inactive.'

'Oh, you can tell me about that later.' He seemed interested but not enough to talk during the rest of the drive.

Jethro pulled into a wider section of the road like a layby. The silence grew deeper as he set the car to standby.

'Okay we're getting out here. Just follow me.'

'Where are we going?'

'Just follow me. And keep your lights off.'

They stepped out of the car. Solace was always thankful for his warm clothing but here he marvelled at its efficacy as they trudged headlong into the swampy landscape. The mist had a vague glow but it only seemed to illuminate itself rather than the landscape. He could see Jethro largely because of the hole he made in the low mist. At times the low level mist seemed to blow apart and leave a gap straight up to the stars.

They walked in silence for a while until Solace realised that he was immediately behind Jethro who had stopped moving. Solace stopped beside him but instinctively said nothing. Jethro held his arm and pointed it to the right, releasing it only a few seconds later after a tiny beam of light burst upon a bank of mist. He began to walk towards the light and Solace followed.

It became clear that the beam of light was a head torch and that somebody else was clambering through the marsh. For what purpose, Solace couldn't even guess. Minutes later a series of other torches appeared near the first. The original light seemed to turn around seeking the source of the new lights, a second or so of frantic roving light giving the impression of surprise or panic.

Jethro began to run, surprisingly fast given the depth of the marsh at this point. Solace ran too, surprised it wasn't harder to do so despite the low viscosity of the marsh liquid. He was briefly but intensely happy lurching forward through the night until he thought about the unknown depths ahead of him. He tried to keep directly behind Jethro in case it was deeper to either side. Fuck knows what they would do when they arrived at the other lights.

Suddenly Jethro switched on his head torch. The beams ahead became shorter and more diffuse as they pointed towards the new light source. Solace switched his on too. The lights ahead began to retreat together although it was difficult to know which direction anybody was moving in. Whatever was going on ahead it felt as if they might have saved somebody from something.

The rest of the run took a minute at a reduced pace and they slowed to a walk when they were close enough to make out the outline of a figure waiting for them.

The figure was small and slight, certainly a woman. She stood looking down at the marsh with her headlight creating a pool of light. In the surrounding nothingness, small areas of light that never carry far enough make everything seem enclosed. The limits of vision the limits of the world itself.

She turned in the direction of their splashing steps and dancing torch beams. The three pools of light connected them as if they were in a room together. Solace and Jethro both pulled their masks aside, letting the thick marsh gases into their lungs unfiltered but revealing what they hoped were friendly faces.

'Are you okay? Do you need help?' asked Jethro.

'Share,' she said.

'He can but I'm unable,' Solace pointed at Jethro.

Seconds passed in silence.

'Thank you. Thank you for chasing them off. There were only two of you and five of them, I didn't know if they'd leave.'

'Thank you. I'm just happy we were able to intervene,' said Solace, only now remembering that he had a gun.

'I came out into the wilderness with the intention of killing myself. I even did my makeup for the occasion. Joked with myself that it was a new style called mortuary chic. I wandered through the marshes like some Shakespearian wench out of her mind with grief. It's comic even to me.'

'Nobody's laughing,' said Jethro. 'You'd be surprised how many people simply walk out into the marsh and disappear. Mainly men though.'

'Do you know those guys?' Solace wasn't sure whether he ought to ask why she wanted to die or to find out about the people they had chased.

'They must have followed me here. There were no vehicles when I arrived. Fucking creeps just started to circle me. They didn't say anything. I never expected to be terrified of strangers whilst trying to kill myself.'

'Your sense of humour is darker than mine,' said Jethro. 'Should we ride back together? We could walk you to your car if it's closer? Ours is about a kilometre or more back the way we came.'

They walked back towards the nearby road to find a car with its doors thrown wide open and aggressive, thumping dance music pouring out. Jethro leaned into the car and turned off the music.

'I like to sit in the front,' said the woman. 'One of you will have to take the back seat.'

'I will,' said Solace. 'I'm sure you two have shared names but what should I call you?'

'Sorry. This is Eve. She thinks you look gentle even if you can't share.'

Solace, pleased, got in the back seat. 'I'm very happy to meet you, Eve.'

They took Eve back to her own flat. She said she was sorry to insult them but she didn't want them to come in because they were men and she was still scared and shaken. It was honest and neither of them took offence. Jethro asked if he could wait outside in the car while she invited some female friends to keep her company and in the end she agreed.

Sitting in the car Solace called Karla.

'I've just had a disturbing experience but without going into too much detail right now can I ask you to check something?'

'You've become very mysterious since you took on the role of investigator. What do you need?'

'Can you track my location half an hour ago, out in the marshes? I was on foot with my friend Jethro and we encountered a woman out there called Eve. She was almost attacked by a group of men. Do you think you could trace and identify those men?'

'Okay I've located your trace. While I'm watching your icon wander through a map, want to tell me what on earth you were doing out there?'

'Difficult to explain,' Solace looked at Jethro who had a confused look on his face. Solace realised he ought to have explained a few things to Jethro before making the call.

'Okay I see you encounter a woman in the marsh now. There's nobody else around though. Not for miles.'

'Shit.'

'Did you notice any detail about them?'

'They were just lights in the dark. The woman was suicidal. They just appeared in the marsh as if they were going to watch her die or something worse.'

'Leave it with me then but see if the woman remembers anything else, if she's not in shock.'

Jethro spoke as soon as Solace hung up. 'Am I part of an investigation now?' His tone was slightly accusatory.

'No, definitely not.' He wanted to say more but didn't want to ruin the rapport that existed between them. 'I came with you for personal reasons. I just couldn't ignore what happened out there.'

'You could have told me you were crew.'

'I'm not.'

'You can't edit, you work with the crew but you're not part of them. Who are you?'

'I feel safe in your car like I'm a sleepy kid being driven home at night by his parents. I like your vibe. We've spent hours together and you've never needed to know more about me. Let's not let that change.'

Jethro was smiling and relaxed. 'Sounds like a declaration of some sort.'

'I sometimes think about sucking your cock when we're in the car.'

'I know, I've seen you looking and guessed. I didn't mind.'

'Good.'

'Do you want to come to my art class? It's on Friday.'

'Yeah, I'd love to actually.'

'Is your friend going to call you back about the guys we saw?'

'Probably not tonight. Best not to mention that to anybody else either, if you don't mind.' Solace looked up and down the street, waiting for the arrival of Eve's friends so they could leave knowing she wasn't alone.

Six

Solace watched Dascha retreating into the inscrutable mists below. He had tried to encourage her to follow Karla's plan but he couldn't persuade her without revealing the big picture. In the end he suggested that the integrity of editors was in question without telling her the details. She understood the ramifications but was far too angry at the thought of people being edited to cooperate. It didn't change her worldview, which already included suspicion of any authority, but it hardened her. She said this was too big to make decisions on alone and she needed to consult. That would take a couple of days to get the information out to all the women and arrange meetings. It was more important than ever not to reveal their group. Solace hadn't told her that Karla knew about them, which meant the authorities she feared knew too. She might as well just call her friends or hold a public meeting. He watched her march through the sleet.

'Why do I get the feeling I've just radicalised Dascha?'

'Just Dascha? When we all get together I promise you there will be direct action.'

'Just don't cut me out of any plans.'

Ren looked at him with questioning eyes but he said nothing more. He wondered if she had guessed that he wasn't giving up all the information. That would make him more loyal to somebody other than her. When she spoke he felt his fears confirmed.

'Are you cutting me out of your plans, Solace?'

He spoke without thinking, wondering what he would say.

'You're always in my plans, babe.' He smiled for many reasons at once. He was shocked that his trust in Ren had evaporated with her single comment. Suddenly a game was being played that made him sick with guilt.

'I have to go back and find out the latest on the case. I'll bring news when I can. Maybe we can stop Dascha from creating a panic.' He left as quickly as he could, trying not to avoid her gaze.

\#

'Where are you?'

'Just arriving. On the plaza now. Why?'

'There's been another one, out in the fields this time.' Karla said, peering out of her window above the domes of Shelter, looking at the tiny figures on the plaza below, one of which was Solace.

'Should I still come up?'

'No. I'll come down to you and we'll take a car out to the scene.' Solace said nothing in reply. 'Solace, no need to come if you don't think you can deal with it.'

'No, no. Come down. I'll call a car.'

Blissfully warm air circulated throughout the car and since neither cared to drive they set the seating to lounge so they could talk comfortably.

'I'm glad we get some time together on the way.'

'Let me update you on our captive as we ride,' said Karla indicating with a gesture that perhaps this was not the private time or place for discussing other matters. 'Dayron and Heidi think that Deek was probably capable of killing before whatever happened to him. They established that the algorithms in his editor are more like notes on how to behave rather than commands that must be obeyed. He's not a puppet, just a kind of mentally butchered human living one day at a time with a set of basic guidelines to replace his recent memories and get him through the day without betraying what he is.'

'So whatever he did, he's still culpable. At least that's something.'

'Dayron said his memories are all ancient and hard to decipher but there's something bizarre about them. Like they don't fit together properly. At the moment he's just working on a kind of memory metadata but he's hoping to resolve them soon and we should know more.'

'If you can ignore the horror of it, it's kind of fascinating,' said Solace wistfully.

Head in hands, Karla looked at Solace. 'I love that you're a dreamer but you're really not getting the implications here.'

'I think I get it. I'm just able to see how interesting it is too.'

'I'm clinging on to reality and here's something that threatens to completely undermine it. I need a distinction between fact and fiction, between the real and imagination. I'm scared that my memories could be edited and refabricated so often it'll be impossible or meaningless to find truth.'

'I know but I can't help being intrigued by the concepts anyway.'

Karla, seeing how relaxed he was, let Solace stare out of the window in silence for the rest of the journey. There was no discomfort in the silence and Karla was still circumspect about speaking too much in locations where she could be surveilled. It was odd, she thought, that as her fears about the integrity of her identity increased so her concerns about surveillance decreased.

As the car pulled up at a layby in the dark Solace seemed to emerge from his daze. The lights inside made the outside a solid black. Karla dimmed the lights and peered out to see where the scene was. Theirs was the only vehicle but drones swam in the air a short distance into the fields. She asked the car to display the drone feeds in a collage. Harsh lights thankfully blanked out some of the detail but it was possible to see globules of flesh splattered across the swaying crops. The body was naked and white against the dark. As she watched, looking for anything unusual, the head raised itself slightly off the ground and collapsed back again with the effort.

'She's alive!' she shouted as she thumped the door release with a fist. Impatience was replaced with caution as she stepped outside and realised the killer might have been disturbed. 'Solace, have you got your gun? Get it ready in case he's still nearby.'

'Shouldn't we wait for the others?'

'She's alive. We have to get to her and protect her. The forensic team are probably still suiting up and packing their kit. I've signalled for backup too but that's likely to be five minutes.' She asked the car to give her a hypothermia pack and it obliged. 'Let me get the drones to do a quick circle sweep then we'll get in there.'

The drones moved swiftly from the victim outwards in ever increasing circles as they hunted for heat signatures or movement. It took seconds to confirm the path was clear then Karla led the way. When they arrived at the victim Karla knelt down and reached out to put a reassuring hand on hers before laying a heated blanket on top of her. She wanted to roll her off the ground onto it but was scared to worsen the injuries. She leaned in close to the woman's face looking for signs of life, hoping she might have something to say. She looked dead, her face slack and blank.

The crops around Karla's head flickered as something small and very fast ripped through them. The drones reacted before Karla could command them, heading rapidly back towards the covered farms. Their search capabilities were excellent but they carried no weapons. Armed automata were forbidden on Liszt. As they approached the buildings they released swarms of tiny drones invisible to Karla and Solace but for the information they relayed back to them.

A moving heat signature that was far too small to be a person wove its way across the mosaic of images. Liszt was rich in many things but not indigenous life, so far as they had been able to determine. No livestock had been brought along for the journey, only an ark of genetic samples for the preservation of species from Earth that was yet to be deployed.

'Low light,' said Karla to her wrist. The drone swarm presented them now with a grainy image of a person keeping low and moving quietly away from them. 'Their suit is retaining all their body heat apart from one small vent.'

'Should we go after them?'

Huge glowing clusters of mist lit from within like explosions of white light in a cloud indicated the approach of vehicles. 'We can now that the forensics team and backup are almost here. Get your gun ready and stay behind me. Don't shoot me in the back.' She thought about waiting for the others but she would be walking towards them anyway. Forensics would head directly to the scene but backup would already be on the drone feed and aware of the shooter's location.

She made sure her suit was fastened properly against the biting cold and trudged towards the farm, her weapon drawn. She didn't want to relink her bracelet to her editor but she wanted direct knowledge of the drone feed rather than having to look at it. She decided bullets were less dangerous than her editor and marched onwards without pairing.

Solace walked behind her with more grace than she would have expected, naturally keeping a rhythm that allowed efficient walking through the marshy field. She felt a brief pleasure at having him here before switching her focus back to catching the killer. One of the vehicles pulled in behind the farm tunnel and sped along to the end, another stopped level with the middle, leaving her and Solace approaching on the other side. The killer could not escape. Should he not have anticipated this result, wondered Karla, knowing that backup was only minutes away once the body was discovered? The risk of getting cornered must have been increased by his decision to take a shot at Karla in the field. And if he was serious about killing Karla he could have made a more concerted effort.

'Something doesn't quite fit here,' she said to herself and the team. 'After years of going without detection we suddenly catch two in a few days. Too easy. Be very careful.'

The drone feed rounded the entrance to the tunnel, moving abruptly from low light grainy images to the brightly lit interior. Rows of plants almost reaching the ceiling above made it a serene and pleasant place. In the middle of a long corridor between the plants stood the killer. He calmly faced the drone and its swarm, raised his gun in front of him and ejected the magazine. The sound of it hitting the cold, hard floor echoed down the feed. The killer stood now with his hands on his head and his legs apart in apparent surrender.

As the team moved in around the killer Karla anticipated the unmasking of the killer in his head to toe thermal suit. There was something primitive but important, she thought, about looking him in the eye. It was not the end of their interaction but the beginning of a new phase. A challenge and an assertion of her dominance over him in this new situation of capture and interrogation. Of course it was too late to prevent an edit on his part so she had no idea what to expect.

The drones showed the team approaching from behind, shouting orders to lie down face down on the ground. The killer complied and was cuffed in that position before being hoisted to his feet again, arms behind his back. His hood was unlocked and peeled back, the team aware that their colleagues were all following the drone feed. It was a woman.

'Dascha!'

Karla turned to look at Solace, 'This is Dascha? Ren's friend?' She disguised her surprise but not her disappointment. Her feeling that something was wrong had not dissipated with this revelation.

'Yes, that's her. I can't believe she committed that crime. Her hatred of these killers is too intense to be faked. More than that, she's shared with Ren before.' As he said that last he looked at Karla as if asking for an explanation.

Naz looked at Solace and back at Karla but didn't ask who he was. They all looked flushed with recent activity despite the time spent driving back to the centre. Dascha was already being boxed up next door, ready for interrogation. The victim was dead and forensics were still on the scene gathering evidence.

'Naz, anything to catch up on about Deek while we wait for Dascha to be prepped?'

'Actually, yes,' he gestured with his bracelet, sending a document to Karla.

She put it straight on the wall opposite so they could all examine the report together.

The report showed that Deek had various memories from his early life with which it had been possible to reconstruct his grim early years. There were clips of key events embedded in the text. They clearly predated the new editing technology and were based not on the events themselves but memories of them, actively remembered at a later date. It gave them a very low integrity, low resolution feel but also an otherworldly temporal logic and occasional unreal physics. They were only watching the visuals projected on a wall but Karla wondered what it would be like to share them and know the other information embedded. When you just viewed visuals rather than sharing properly you missed out on all the parts a brain adds to stimuli. The direct visual data was there and each sharer would fill in the blanks in their own way. The subject's visual focus would shift with some faces partially formed, here showing eyes pin sharp, there showing lips moving, peripheral vision blurred and haunting figures shifting in the background. The procedural notes showed that the memories had not been shared by the technicians either, due to their malformation.

They watched from Deek's point of view as a wiry, shirtless man reached down and slapped him across the face repeatedly. There were other instances of physical abuse, first by the wiry man and then by others too. The abuse was predominantly torture but also sexual and the graphic memories were of precisely the sort many people choose to edit out of their heads. This guy had instead dug up his oldest, worst memories and deliberately recorded them for posterity. A glutton for punishment. Karla wondered if he missed his abusers.

'I recognise that face.' Naz leaned in closer, pausing the footage. 'He's still alive and well today, I can tell you that.'

'Who is he?'

'I don't know his name but I see him around the gallery district behind Warszawa sometimes. He's younger now, of course, but it's him.'

'These are memories of memories. Unreliable. We can't be sure this actually happened.'

'Could these be memories of dreams or fantasies?' Solace still lacked current knowledge when it came to editing.

'Impossible to tell I'm afraid. Naz, get Reuben and Natsuki to work on this guy. He may have erased this already but let's work on the assumption that surprise is useful just in case.'

Naz wandered into the corner of the room to call Reuben and Natsuki. In cases like this there was a moral issue to consider: the abuse of the individual's right to privacy through enforced sharing versus the perceived likelihood of guilt. In this case the crime was serious and the evidence was compelling, on the face of it anyway, so he would be zapped and boxed.

On the wall opposite the horror story of Deek's memories continued. He was a withdrawn child at school. Children moved around him, excited and high pitched, while he remained static, occasionally stared at but mostly ignored. Soon the bullying came too but he was already accustomed to violence and he showed himself willing to fight back.

'Dascha's ready for interrogation.' Dayron put his head round the door to tell them rather than use his bracelet.

'How much more is there to this report?'

'You're almost at the end. It seems to stop at the point he finishes his studies. By that time he seems to have suffered silently for years at the hands of pretty much everybody he meets. It's brutal but then it just stops and the next memory is the murder. Did you see that we didn't share though?'

'Yes, malformed memories.'

'Yup, still possible to share them but who knows what kind of shit they'll put in your head? At the end of the report we also talk about the possibility of the whole thing being a work of fiction. In particular there are some memories that don't seem to belong to the same subject. Obviously they're degraded and difficult to read but it seemed to us that in a couple of places the subject was a girl.'

'Okay so if that's true then it could be that none of the memories are Deek's.'

'Entirely possible. The editor is tampered with, as we said.'

'So we could be leading a totally fabricated life. Born yesterday with implanted memories of a fictitious past.' She thought about the replicants in Bladerunner, one of her favourite science fiction movies of all time. She let images from the film drift around in her head for a few seconds.

'Well *his* history might be fabricated. Not ours though. We don't have editors like his.'

'Have you checked?' She watched his face just hang like a glitch. Obviously he hadn't checked. 'Anyway, the guy could be a blank that gets filled up with memories as required and then off he goes to lead the life they, whoever they are, have designed for him.'

'Not quite as simple as that. Knowledge remains. And yes knowledge is remembered just like other things are but our editing tech is by design focused on manipulating stimuli or sharing experiences. It's much less well equipped to go digging around in our heads for knowledge. I mean I can only tell if he knows how to speak Chinese if I find a significant memory of him using it or maybe learning it in adulthood. I'm not able to tell you how many Chinese characters he has stored away in there.'

'Of course, that's kind of what I meant by blank.'

'Okay, just clarifying.'

'Right let's go and see Dascha,' she walked towards the doorway Dayron was still hovering in. 'Wait, one more thing. Knowledge persists but how about personality?'

'All the structures in his brain, all the connections made based on his biology and life experience, they're all still there. In theory he's the same guy he was but without certain issues. For example, if he was frequently angered by remembering his childhood and you erased it you would find out how much of his personality was permanently prone to anger and how much of that anger was just triggered by the memory directly. It's not a simple question really and you'd probably have to experiment to find out.'

'Pretty unethical experiments to perform though so I'm guessing nobody's done them and written a paper on it.'

'Correct.'

'But he's still a free agent, even if his personality is partly synthetic he has free will.'

'Absolutely. We obviously can't be sure about the memories yet though, it's only a strong suspicion.'

'Okay now we can go and talk to Dascha.'

\#

Solace sat at home looking out the window and thinking. A car passed far below and he thought of Jethro.

Dascha had turned out to be a husk of her former self. Wiped just like Deek but also implanted with the same memories of childhood abuse Deek had in his head. Not just similar ones but identical ones. Some sort of construct rather than a real person. Apart from the technical challenges of doing this, which were not slight, there was the question of why.

Did they choose Dascha because of her investigation? Did they want to send a message or was it a taunt? Was the message that anybody, even a defender of women, could commit these acts?

Karla had ordered an investigation into her whereabouts over the last few days but there were no results and perhaps not much expected given her desire to hide her own location and leave her bracelet behind so often.

His phone projected a dancing image of Karla and he picked it up. 'Hey, what news?'

'The victim was part of Dascha's organisation. Probably somebody she went to meet recently to talk to about her investigation. Both of them would have been without their bracelets so difficult to locate.'

'It's worrying that Dascha could be made to do this. She was volatile but to become the thing she hated most, that's just incredible.'

'I don't even know what to make of it.'

'What do your bosses think about it?' It occurred to Solace that this thing would not be good for public morale and he wondered if those in higher authority might try to suppress news of it.

'Strange you mention that. There's a void of influence there. They listen but don't take further action beyond my own. It's been puzzling me.'

'My buzzer just went. Must be Ren at the door.' Without looking at the video feed, he told the flat to let her up. 'I find myself thinking about you, Karla.'

'Go entertain your guest.'

Seven

Solace had arrived early at Jethro's art class and watched a trickle of people enter the large room over the last half hour. All of them knew each other to some extent and a few of them cast glances in his direction but moved off without saying anything. He wondered if they had tried to share with him and been irritated with a lack of reaction from him. Unlike them, he didn't get a mental ping when somebody attempted contact. The room settled down with most people having found their space alone or near one other person. Obviously a group for loners and introverts. He thought back to his early days of hanging out in the local library, its aisles full of paperbacks and unhealthy people with no money.

Jethro arrived at the back of the room and walked to the front where Solace was sitting. He put a heavy hand on his shoulder and said hello, smiling as he took a seat. 'I'm glad you came.'

'I have no idea what's going on,' Solace spoke in the hushed voice he used in quiet rooms full of people, 'but it's good to see you. Nobody has said a word to me so far.'

Jethro laughed, 'Why would they? You're the weird guy sitting at the front not sharing.'

'True. I bring it on myself, this social isolation.'

Jethro squeezed his shoulder again, 'Aw. The class will start soon. Today it's a life drawing session. Have you done it before?'

'Not for a century or so.'

'Well, you'll probably be rubbish then but do your best.'

A tall thin man with curiously small feet passed round what

looked like paper attached to boards. Jethro called it 'repaper' but gave no explanation. Charcoal too was something other than the original version but indistinguishable to Solace anyway. After he had handed the last boards and charcoal out, the man headed to the centre of the room where there was a small raised platform and began to undress. He had an interesting body, Solace thought, because of the visibility of every tendon and muscle beneath his low fat surface.

'Shit, he's facing the other way,' Solace was disappointed to be looking at the man's back.

'We can move if you don't like looking at his bony arse. You want to go to the side over there or in the middle so you can see his cock?'

Solace wasn't sure if Jethro wanted to see the cock or if he was being considerate to Solace on the assumption that he wanted to see it. 'Yup, let's walk past all these people and sit where we can see the cock.'

A couple of hours later the class was finished and Jethro asked Solace if he wanted to go for a drink. They headed out towards Warszawa, deciding on the way between coffee shop and bar. They chose bar and headed inside. Solace felt a small thrill of expectation and possibilities as they walked towards the bar, taking in the people looking their way. They took a seat at the bar and ordered beer.

'I was surprised that you went to art classes. It didn't fit with my image of you for some reason.'

'What image is that?' Jethro often sounded confrontational to Solace but he had learned it was just a challenging directness about the man.

'I don't know but it was a surprise.'

'Well I hope it was a pleasant one. Anyway, there's something fundamentally relaxing about drawing. Particularly drawing naked humans.'

'Definitely. I remember my old art teacher from school got me to draw a statue of Aphrodite. He knew I would enjoy recreating her curves.'

'I don't think we do enough of that sort of thing on Liszt. Ancient things that give us pleasure and connect us to our primitive roots. If I could find a cave I'd spit paint through my fingers onto the walls by candlelight.'

'I'd be right there with you making haunting tunes by banging bones on the stalactites. It would be one of the more normal things to do here.' Solace imagined the life model picking his way naked over rocks in the cave, tracing a path worn smooth by millennia of foot traffic. 'Tens of thousands of years doing the same thing on the same planet then bang, we're on another world light years away.'

Jethro raised his glass to the light, 'Still drinking beer though.'

'A time like ours must have been unimaginable to the people in those caves. The future is always stranger than any you can invent.'

'I bet they had a notion of things being eternal but not of change and upheaval. To them things probably didn't change much during each lifetime.' Jethro nodded at the bartender for more beer.

'The eternal but not deep time. It was only when we understood the formation of rocks and fossils that we started to understand those long timescales. Not that we can really comprehend them.'

'No, we have to resort to poetic language.'

'Although we're changing our understanding of time by living longer. There's no telling how long we might last now.' Solace was optimistic but hadn't bothered to find out about the science behind the anti-senescence treatments. It was another item on his long list of things to explore.

'Living longer brings its own problem, not least the mental changes. Memory defines a life. So many memories are edited, gaps created, so much lost that a sense of identity morphing emerges. Creating yourself turns out to be an emotional trip. People continually reinvent themselves as they run away from things they don't want to face. The old them fades over time and becomes a death in the family that nobody can talk about. Repressed grief surfaces as pain and tears at random moments and is immediately suppressed with edits and drugs. Being long-lived also creates issues of boredom, existential depression, concerns over the future.'

'Is that how it affects you personally?'

'Some of it, not all. I don't edit. Ever. I share with people when it's expected of me but I never edit my experiences or my memories. I haven't lost the man I used to be but I have to make a real effort to keep him alive.'

'I feel the need to tell you Jethro, you've made a huge impression on me as a person.'

#

Yost enjoyed driving. He was older than most, as was Yvonne. Older even than Solace and Karla and somehow that decade longer on Earth felt far more significant than 50 years extra in space. They were out beyond the farms, circling them on the orbital road that connected all of the spokes from the centre. They were looking for any sign of activity in areas where bodies had been found recently. Yost thought now about driving his old Citroen through French country roads on the way back to the city after a weekend away. The tastes and smells of France filled his nostrils like happiness. These moments of euphoria came to him sometimes and he thought of them as gifts to be shared. He broadcast this heady second into the ether.

Yvonne smiled at him, country air and coffee in her nose, at just the moment he jerked the wheel in horror at the sudden and unexpected taste of human flesh. Deciding that the driver would be unable to turn this manoeuvre into anything other than a crash, the car took back control and drove itself safely to a halt by the side of the road. Yost shoved his door open and vomited in the dirt. The car asked if they needed assistance but Yost ignored it, closed the door and turned to Yvonne.

'Somewhere nearby they're sharing the taste of human flesh on broadcast. I don't know if they picked up on my own signal. We might still have the element of surprise.'

Yvonne signalled for stealth assistance and local drone swarm feeds to locate the nearest warm bodies. Yost was aware that the car's presence might alert the suspects but didn't want to move it until he knew their location and how to avoid them. He had been driving in stealth mode using the low light camera anyway so they still had a chance.

Drone feeds finally arrived, they saw one of the farm tunnels ahead and on their left was a couple of degrees warmer than the others. The vaguest of movement inside. It was too close for comfort. Yost decided the safest thing was to let the car roll gently down off the far side of the road where it would be hidden. The car itself was silent other than the unavoidable hum of power like a cathode ray tube in the dark and the gentle displacement of slush.

Around them in the dark gathered a great concentration of drones of all sorts. Drones controlled directly by humans were allowed to carry a non-lethal pacifier designed to bring about virtually instant unconsciousness. The controllers back in Shelter now had to devise a strategy to pacify as many of the suspects as they could simultaneously or risk losing valuable memories. They couldn't afford to wait long as every action could bring them closer to detection.

The smallest of drones, invisible to the human eye, gathered by windows and relayed the patchwork of images back. Three dimensional models were constructed, distances measured, probabilities calculated. For the second time in days the crew were preparing to storm a farm tunnel.

The distribution of people in the room was such that it would be difficult to pacify them all at the same time. Back in their tower overlooking Shelter, the crew decided to wait and record some of the current broadcast sharing in case their pacification had a poor result. Drones hovered in the vicinity, absorbing thoughts they didn't understand for subsequent retrieval and study.

Yost and Yvonne had turned sharing off for the wait to avoid nausea at the memories being broadcast. The taste of flesh had been intense, Yost told Yvonne. So intense that he could barely wait until after his testimony before deleting it from his memory.

The drones were finally all in position for entry to the transparent tunnel at the optimum points. Clustered on all sides but also above the structure their entry would be timed as a group, their pacifiers automatically focused on pre-selected targets and their human pilots ready to press the trigger at the appropriate moment. The time had arrived.

Yost switched sharing back on as the order was given and leaned away from the drone feed screens to get a view out of the window at the real scene. There was nothing to see at first, the tiny drones plunging at high speed into the tunnel and seeking their targets. Tiny facets of reflected light shone briefly against a black sky before jets of warm air ejected from the holes created a rapidly cooling cloud. Inside there were shapes like people falling heavily to the floor on all sides. Some figures remained standing, moving within, as drones within the space neutralised the crew drones before they could achieve their targets. It was unlikely that the group had enough drones to resist the torrent of crew drones that now descended upon them in a miniature war of attrition.

Yost and Yvonne exited the car in case they were needed to help capture the remaining men. Even as their feet hit the slush the men were already down.

Yvonne shared a vivid experience of cinnamon toast with Yost. He turned to her, 'That's sweet of you but actually the thought of food right now still makes me want to heave.'

'Sorry, I thought it would take the taste away.'

'You know, just before the entry I caught something. They call themselves the Virgin Club. Sinister pricks.'

#

Yost came out of his testimony box looking a whole lot better for having divested himself of the taste of flesh. Karla was there to greet him. 'Good result, Yost.'

'I'd like to say I was super vigilant but it was just luck that I was casually sharing thoughts of home as I drove along.' He rolled his tongue across his teeth underneath his top lip.

'Well a result is a result,' said Karla. There had been public debates about surveillance drones listening in on a random sample of people as they flew around the colony to detect illegal activity but it had failed the vote. It was seen as a first step towards machines controlling people and that didn't go down well in a colony full of independent, rugged people.

'I suppose the ones that didn't get zapped in the first wave had time to wipe?'

'They had the time but they didn't. Quite a surprise. They're in the box now being interrogated.' She sipped her tea, pensive. 'I didn't want to get a full dose of those memories,' she said to explain why she wasn't there now. As she said it, she decided she was shirking and went back towards the interrogation room still in use.

'I'm going to head home, if that's okay,' Yost called down the corridor at her retreating back.

Naz looked up as Karla came entered the viewing gallery. 'Hey, interesting development.'

'What's that then?'

'These guys all have a huge number of graphic memories of murder, some of them the same as each other. I'm pretty certain they're from other people. I mean, I can't rule out that these guys aren't murderers themselves but these memories seem like a collection.'

'So what are these guys – storage?' Even as she said it the horror of it began to sink in. 'They're a library of murders?'

'I think we interrupted a sharing party for murderers and their fans.'

'What sort of context do we have?'

'Unfortunately they must have wiped a fair bit of that. Another one of their pre-defined wipe orders but one that left the crimes intact this time. I can't figure out why.'

'You're telling me it's like these guys deleted their personal memories but kept a store of murders?'

'We'll have to ask Heidi when she's finished. This is getting into territory where I can't give you an answer really.'

'Where's Dayron?' She saw that only Heidi was in the room with the boxed men.

'He's probably still throwing up.'

Karla felt a little pang of affection for Dayron, who was starting to remind her a little of Solace. He had no stomach for this either. 'Hopefully we'll get more out of the ones we caught unawares.'

There were twenty seven captives in total. The thought of their stored memories flowing through Heidi on her own, tough as she obviously was, made Karla feel guilty. She walked towards the entrance to the room determined to support her efforts.

\#

Stimulants served a primarily recreational purpose on Liszt but Karla sometimes popped a little something on long stints at the office. Heidi seemed full of energy that came from nowhere so she discreetly ensured she could keep up with her. It had the unfortunate consequence of intensifying some of the experience but Karla endured it to stay awake. An entire day passed as they pushed on through the endless stream of men. Certain concepts had emerged and they sought to confirm these in each subject before determining a further, deeper study of them all at a later date.

These men proved to be part of something called Virgin Club. They didn't just wipe memories so they could avoid detection. No, they wanted each new kill to give them the same intense thrill as their first kill. Previously they had to sink to deeper levels of depravity, take greater risks to get their high. Their solution was just like that of the lovers who forget each other every few months so they can discover each other afresh. That was the first thing they found about the men.

The second was the idea of competition amongst killers. The narcissistic thrill of sharing a new crime masterfully executed, a new beautiful victim, the cruellest torture, all of it applauded by an adoring audience killing with you for the first time. Rock stars.

The third concept was that of the library. Deleting was one thing but they didn't want to lose their back catalogue forever. They needed to retain the memories somewhere for later retrieval and sharing. Actually committing murder carried a lot of risks but storing that memory was a further risk that endured long past the kill itself like a trophy waiting to be discovered under the floorboards. There seemed to be some way of allocating the task of library storage for a time, like serving a tour of duty. Never just one man of course, in case of death or capture. These individuals were expected to avoid too much personal exposure during their tour and certainly to avoid sharing. They were stored, fed and watered like living media.

Heidi was fascinated by the library as it contravened some of the technical aspects of the editor. Normal people can share their own memories but you can't record somebody else's memory, only your experience of it. Somehow these memories were being shared as a first person experience. Heidi had data sent to Dayron for investigation while they continued with their initial analysis.

The fourth element of this horror story led back to Deek. Partially deleted, cut back to the original first green shoots of a killer, programmed to carry out crimes and record them for the library. More astonishing still was that multiple participants carried out different parts of the crime. One to abduct, another to transfer to another location, another to kill, another to dispose of the evidence. Choreographed from somewhere unknown by an entity that couldn't be identified. Nobody knew who organised the whole affair.

Karla couldn't work out if this was just a way to reduce the risks of capture or if it was somehow more fundamental. She was approaching the point where sleep would force itself upon her despite additional doses of narcotics.

Eight

Natsuki walked through the crowds slowly, taking in more than most as she did. Reuben followed a similar path on the other side of the street. Between them flowed a river of the artistically inclined out on a night of culture and indulgence. Higher than average levels of editing and drug use made them peculiarly oblivious to the crew but hyper aware of each other. Natsuki felt like a sociologist studying some subculture back on Earth. Her audio was flooded with their obnoxiously loud conversations but it didn't bother her. She let it all wash in, through and out the other side like a calm area in rapids. The man whose face Naz had recognised in Deek's memories had been identified as Sugar Fearless. He was some twenty metres ahead with his crowd of sycophants encircling him.

They had been watching Sugar for the whole evening. He certainly didn't hide himself away, refuse to share or otherwise act like a guilty man. They slipped in and out of his vicinity, catching snippets of phrases, feeling the heat of bodies around them, catching the occasional stray share of witty phrases, flamboyantly posed situations, new flavours of emotion. The whole gallery district was like a festival of self-obsessed artistic creation. Everybody was part of the show. Everybody except Natsuki and Reuben who didn't fit in at all.

Natsuki motioned to Reuben discretely to move in closer again. It looked to her as if he might be preparing to leave the district and head for some after party somewhere. She thought about whether it would be best to pick him up now or wait and see what else they might learn. As she walked she picked up a share from one of his crowd, a woman lying on her back looking up at his sweating face as he fucked her. Natsuki felt his dick inside her as she approached him in the street. It disgusted her as she remembered his face in the visuals from Deek's cesspit mind. As soon as she was in range, she hit him on the side of the head as hard as she could with the heel of her hand. She saw shock on Reuben's face as Sugar collapsed onto the ground and the people around him cleared a space with their gasps. The woman didn't stop sharing her fuck but Natsuki had tuned out already.

Boxed and looking confused, Sugar recovered consciousness. Natsuki sat in the observation lounge while Naz and Reuben were ready to interview him. On the screen the words plucked from his editor suddenly appeared.

Intensify physical sensation of restriction. Increase lighting and contrast. Record all.

'Sorry, that won't work in the box,' Reuben's voice had always sounded like chocolate to Natsuki. 'But an interesting choice nonetheless. Most people try to delete stuff at this point.'

'Why on earth would I delete anything?'

Naz sighed, 'We saw you abusing a child, you pervert.'

Sugar stared in return, looking from Naz to Reuben and back again. 'No. You didn't.'

'I could show you. I might in a moment. Jog your memory. First though, we're going to take a look inside your head so if you want to chat about anything now go ahead.'

'Chat? What are you fucking talking about?'

'Where did you get your accent from?' Reuben had been dying to comment on it all night.

'I hybridised it from various twencen European sources. It's rather fun.'

'Actually, it is. Kind of non-gendered and camp. You're quite a flamboyant character.' Reuben agreed with him. His neutral attitude began to infect Natsuki who felt her anger fading. She never edited during investigations or she would have disposed of the unpleasant emotion long before now.

'I haven't seen you in the quarter, have I?'

'No. I'm not interesting enough to inhabit your world.'

'No, perhaps not.'

'We really do have footage of you abusing a child. That wasn't something we just made up. Do you genuinely have no memory of it?'

It was likely that he had absolutely no memory of the events, thought Natsuki in her observation exile, but that didn't make him innocent.

'Not many things disgust me but that does. I pride myself on being open to pretty much any and every experience but I would never harm somebody, far less a child. You know, Fearless isn't my given name. I changed it a long time ago because that's what everybody called me. Fearless. Most likely to be first in line for a new experience. First to jump right in. Aesthete and thrill seeker without the machismo. Show me what you have.'

Naz got the footage ready, 'You talk a good game Sugar.'

Sugar watched in silence as the images flickered over the screen. There was his face, older in the ship days but unmistakable. When it stopped Sugar appeared more serious.

'Computer generated fabrication. Share it with me.'

'It's not a normal shared memory. It seems to be some sort of degraded copy implanted in another person's head. We're not sure that it's safe to share.' As he said it, Naz had a slightly guilty look as if he knew his evidence could be flawed.

'So you're prepared to convict me on the basis of some bizarre constructed memory that you're all too chicken to share. Pathetic. Just share it with me now.' Sugar was matter of fact and insistent.

'Because I don't particularly like you or care about you,' said Naz, 'I'm going to treat that as consent. I hope there's no damage as a result of this.'

He wants to know what it's like to be a child abused by him, thought Natsuki watching him. He's more interested in the experience than proving his innocence. Sharing can't prove anything to us anyway because it's not his memory. She felt like a participant in his lust for a new thrill.

He didn't close his eyes for the share but lay there boxed and motionless for the short time it took to transport him back a century in time and light years away. They had watched on the screen as events unfolded but now it was blank.

'Sugar?'

'It feels genuine. I think it's a real memory. I have no recollection of it at all but if it is indeed me then I deserve whatever punishment is coming my way.'

#

'I was thinking of making cinnamon toast later.'

'Sounds tasty. Is that your plan for the evening?'

Just ask me if you can come round, thought Karla, I know you want to. 'That's just the late night snack part. The rest is free.'

'Maybe I could come round and we could catch up.'

'Hurry up. And bring some red wine.'

Solace looked a little lost standing in the doorway as if he wasn't sure how to greet her. I summoned you here and yet still you're filled with doubt, thought Karla. She took control of the situation, kissing him on the lips and pulling him inside by the arm.

'Thanks for bringing the wine. I'm in the mood for a traditional drink even if it came from a lab rather than a vineyard.'

'We can pretend we're in France together.'

'Together?'

'Well, you know, in the same place at the same time.'

Karla turned to face him. She looked him in the eye with what she hoped was a look that challenged him to stop playing games.

'That look is telling me to cut the shit, isn't it?' he asked.

She kept looking, letting a little smile escape.

'Are we falling in love again after all these years? Because I feel that way.'

'Yes! We are!' she almost shouted in her excitement. She laughed and kissed him. He kissed her back and they played the part of desperate first time lovers trying to get to the bedroom whilst stripping frantically. They made it to the living room at least.

Karla looked over to see Solace was lying on his back staring at the ceiling. 'Always afterwards the guilt arrives. You don't have to feel guilty for living your life. Did you promise her you'd always be with her? Did you even promise monogamy?'

'You don't want to be monogamous?'

'Stop asking me for permission, stop trying to find out what I want. You have to think about what you want.' In fact Karla had never particularly cared about sexual monogamy but she did care about emotional intimacy. She didn't think it was possible to be in love with two people at once unless you were all part of a single unit and she didn't want to share with Ren. She had grown to dislike Ren, despite now knowing her. She was aware of her probable bias but still she disliked Ren. 'Listen. You wanted this and you still want it so don't start staring into the void and thinking about her. Be here with me.'

'I do love you, Karla. I've been feeling myself drifting away from Ren but the sex kept dragging me back.'

'And now that we've fucked, after all these years apart, the veil has lifted a little and you can see us both clearly. Her advantage is gone. Aren't people simple creatures at heart?' She said it without sarcasm or irritation.

'I still feel guilty even though I'm certain I've done the right thing for me. She was so good to me when I woke up.'

'I know. I was right there for you too but you cut me out. You couldn't see me, blinded by the sex appeal of a woman a mere century or so younger than me.'

He laughed, 'She really does feel very young. Isn't it remarkable that such things still make any sense at our age?'

'Did you feel like a teenager coming round here with your bottle of wine?' She smiled at her own memories of being a student back on Earth.

'I did. Excited, nervous and wondering what might happen.'

'Maybe there's a way we can keep that feeling forever.' She said it wistfully, knowing that edited lives didn't always work out as expected.

The ambient temperature was set high in Karla's flat and they slept on the sunken floor with a sea of cushions. When they woke up they lay there together looking out the window while Karla updated him on developments in the case. Although as she said it wasn't really a case anymore. It had morphed into an enquiry about the nature of life and people on Liszt. And it had frightening implications about the security of their computer network, which had never before been in question.

'There are rumours going around the colony now that we've caught the murderer. It's our policy to be as open as possible so long as we don't compromise the investigation so in this case I have to keep quiet. But I don't like it.'

'There are too many people involved to keep it quiet forever. And the ramifications are too enormous to keep silent about forever.'

She thought about that but was distracted by his dick hardening against her leg.

#

Heidi watched intently over Dayron's shoulder as he methodically moved the image map on the screen, searching for confirmation of their theory about Sugar. They were looking for signs of tampering with his editor. They had already completed checks on the programs, finding nothing out of the ordinary, and now they sought hardware modifications. Starting with the assumption that it might resemble whatever had been done to Deek, they targeted specific areas. The first had yielded nothing but now as the image slid across the screen there were some of those mysterious little nodules familiar to them from Deek's unit.

Heidi and Dayron exchanged glances but said nothing. It was obvious that the recent series of disturbing events had a history reaching back many decades. Heidi could see the hairs on Dayron's arm standing on end. She put a hand on his shoulder and felt his muscles respond to the welcome touch. There was more to investigate and he carried on scanning.

Most of the modifications to Deek's editor were absent from Sugar's. The obvious conclusion was that Sugar was an early attempt to modify editors, perhaps an experiment long since abandoned. There was of course a possibility that there were some people with all of the modifications and others with just one or two of them. Maybe some people are like pawns and others like rooks or bishops, thought Heidi. How many of them might be out there? Who could be doing this? Does Sugar know about this modification?

Heidi called a sleepy-looking Karla and explained their discovery. Karla seemed particularly pensive upon hearing the news. Heidi felt she was less sure of herself than usual, asking many of the same questions that circulated in Heidi's head. These questions needed answers although it wasn't clear how to find them so now much more analysis was required. Heidi didn't ask what would happen to Sugar. In fact they couldn't yet tell what function the nodules on the editors served and that reverse engineering exercise would take some time. For all they knew, Sugar could have been a puppet.

So now they had multiple subjects to study a wealth of data could be gathered quickly. They had Deek and now his accomplices – some of them anyway. Then Sugar took them back decades to a previous age, showing what could be a prototype of their devices. Physically, there was much to study and learn. But there was a whole other strand involving the memories themselves. There was the possibility that the men had other things in common that were nothing to do with the editors.

As she thought about it, Heidi felt like she was investigating a mystery whilst discovering some real science but she was also terrified by the whole thing. As a woman on Liszt, she hadn't felt safe for many years but now she felt uncomfortable being home alone. She couldn't imagine going home without Dayron by her side and even then she was hyper aware of her surroundings and any sign of danger.

#

Yost didn't turn on the lights, letting the wan light illuminate the room for a while. It was faint enough that everything appeared monochromatic. The subtle lighting rendered everything different shades of grey with occasional bright edges, glass surfaces graduated from white to black. This winter twilight is so beautiful, he thought. He imagined the men they caught, pictured them walking the streets with all the people he knew, all the women he loved and cared about. He thought about them targeting one of those women and following her. Maybe they would follow her for weeks or maybe they were opportunistic but ultimately there would be an attack. He wondered what it was like to attack a woman. A beautiful woman whose flesh he wanted to touch. These horrible thoughts would be explained, experienced even, through the study of the captive killers.

He heard Yvonne waking up in the next room. Small noises of covers being cast aside and footsteps on thick carpet. He turned his head and saw with dark adapted eyes the naked form of Yvonne approaching, her hand at her face as she yawned. As she came closer she was startled by his presence.

'Oh, what are you doing standing naked in the dark? You scared the shit out of me!'

'Sorry. I was just looking out the window and thinking.'

'With a raging hardon.' It was an observation rather than a question.

He looked down at himself, previously unaware of his erection. 'Yes, so I see.'

'What were you thinking about?' Yvonne smiled coquettishly.

'Oh I don't know. The train of thought is gone now. Nothing important.'

He walked towards her, picked her up so she straddled his hips, and walked back towards the bedroom.

#

Heidi and Dayron had been poring over their work for days with little sleep in a frantic attempt to work things out as quickly as possible. As Karla said, there was no telling whether the killers were all captured or if they had just caught a handful from a larger group. They needed to find out how this whole thing worked in order to prevent further killings. Dayron had told her last night that he worried if he slept another woman would be killed in the night. Neither of them had wanted to edit out the feelings, now growing suspicious of their own editors. Now they were fuelled by coffee and drugs, not for the first time that week either.

They were using pattern recognition software and a huge database of behavioural information going back over a century to guide their analysis. They had also, with Karla's authority, recruited the assistance of the leading psychologist from Liszt's only university. Ray had studied the data in preparation for their call.

'There's a kind of psychopathy at work but it's in conflict. There's no doubt he has a moral system developed long ago but now he doesn't follow it because he feels it deep down or has guilt. I think he follows his moral code like reading a map. It's just information about the location of right and wrong.' Ray seemed fully engaged in the conversation, leaning forward into the camera, focused and eyes wide. 'But I don't think he was born that way.'

'What makes you think that?' asked Heidi.

'The moral code is far too well developed. It's as if he was a normal person and some parts of him have become disconnected.'

'I've sometimes wondered what's to stop a psychopath from editing empathy into his emotional world,' Dayron wondered aloud.

'They probably can but they would have to do so deliberately. Anyway, I think it's more worrying that the rest of us have the ability to switch off our empathy if we want to. But that's a side issue. What I'm talking about here is that since the advent of editing, psychology has become a fractured subject. There are those who used to practice psychotherapy through prescription drugs which were like crude hammers applied to very delicate and complex problems often resulting in further damage. I believe editing to be rather like that but I have very little data to go on because people no longer come to us with psychological problems in the same numbers as before. Now the subject is largely academic. The primary source of data I have is in analysing public behaviours and in sharing experiences with others. Of course there's some rich data there but I don't get the really damaged people unless I stumble across them.'

Heidi didn't want to interrupt but she was already forgetting the point of the explanation. 'Sorry, what does this have to do with Sugar? Are you telling me you can't explain because you don't have enough data?'

'What I'm saying is I've never had unlimited access to such a subject's memory. Your forced sharing has given me this access whereas Sugar has kept a lot of himself hidden even when sharing. Quite adept at it too. So here we are finally coming to the point. Imagine a normally functioning person creates a set of opinions and moral codes as they grow up. Then imagine something breaks and although they still have all of that knowledge, hold those opinions, they also feel no particular reason to be bound by them. They continue as before, freewheeling as it were, but if some situation should present a moral dilemma we might suddenly find them acting out of character. They might not realise it themselves until the dilemma presents itself. They might then rationalise their odd behaviour in order to preserve their self-image.'

'He doesn't know he's an evil prick,' said Dayron, 'because he used to be a nice guy, is that what it boils down to?'

'Look,' said Ray looking flustered and talking a little more quickly, 'I'm trying to describe something that nobody on Liszt has had the opportunity to study before. I'm telling you frankly, most people studying this field are only concerned with how to manage emotions through editors to reach some kind of peak happiness. It's like a chronic hedonism blinding us to everything else.'

'I'm sure Dayron didn't mean to upset you,' she looked across at Dayron who raised a hand to apologise, 'but are you saying that nobody really knows anything anymore because everybody is too focused on this miracle cure of editing?'

'Yes, pretty much. What I don't understand is that in the past the companies that made drugs profited from their sale and used appalling practices to continue doing so but here we have no money so what's the driver for editing?'

Dayron laughed. 'The users love it! That's what drives it. Press a button get pleasure.'

'Yes, yes, I know that, but why the official sanction, the continued pushing of the technology as virtually mandatory? Who benefits from that and how?' Ray was intense and remained so seconds after he finished speaking into the camera. Eventually his flushed face relaxed.

Heidi was reminded of earlier conversations with Karla. Who was editing computer records?

'Taking a little step back to Sugar for a moment, if it's purely an intellectual duty to be moral then what would stop him if he became angry? Don't strong emotions always trump logic?' Heidi knew he might edit down his emotions but saw no reason why he would bother if he felt expressing them would be more fulfilling.

'Oddly, I think it's his desire to be true to his vision of himself and his life as a work of art.' Ray was calm again.

'He doesn't mind being punished for something because the punishment is a new experience to add to his masterpiece?' She had wondered something similar herself and was pleased to have her thoughts confirmed. 'Maybe he even sees himself as a tragic martyr.'

'Very likely. Poor persecuted guy, battling against the odds. That would preserve is own view of himself as one of the god guys.'

'Doesn't sound like he's thinking very far ahead though. His masterpiece would come to an end pretty quickly if he was found guilty of child abuse.' Dayron often brought practicalities back into discussions like this.

'Maybe he imagines he'll be allowed to record his final moments before deletion. That he'll then have a fantastic end to his story, that after his personality is erased the new him will be able to start a new story all over again.' Ray was expressive, his gestures sweeping in and out of shot as he spoke.

'Should we tell him that his whole life story would be deleted from existence?' asked Heidi.

'Only if you want him to stop co-operating. But listen, you're not telling me the whole story. This Sugar isn't the only one is he?'

'No,' she said.

'Well, he's the only one of this specific type,' corrected Dayron.

'The others are far more complex,' Heidi watched Ray's eyes widen as she spoke. 'I'll send you the data now.'

'Now that I've proved my competence?'

Heidi explained the rest of the story to him. The killers, the editor modifications, the strange collusion between them, the gatherings in private places to share their killings. She watched Ray drink it in with his eyes, seeming to gasp deeper and with more passion at every new fact she revealed. By the time they ended the call she knew he would work night and day until he could work no more. She liked him and wished Dayron had been a little more sensitive in his comments.

Nine

Solace answered the buzzer and was confronted with an image of Ren's face, somewhat imploring. 'Where have you been, Solace?'

'Come in, come in,' he unlocked the door downstairs and began untangling his thoughts as he waited for her to come up in the lift and appear at his door. He had taken this girl, he still thought of her as a girl, to the brink of a long term relationship and here he was becoming detached. She seemed to be of another time and another sort. He had found his own place in this era and, no longer feeling like an alien, started to see her with more clarity.

He opened the door, 'I hear the pitter patter of your little lady feet.'

She stood in the doorway, looking like she might be on the verge of tears. 'Where the hell have you been? And what the fuck is going on with the investigation?'

'Straight to the point as ever,' he turned away into his flat, making her follow.

'Solace! Since you told me about Dascha I've been really worried and you just disappear.'

He knew she was right. He had virtually abandoned her, thinking of her only in a sexual way from time to time. 'From the moment I met you, you were as tough as anybody I ever knew. You didn't let me feel a second of self-pity. I suppose I think of you as self-sufficient. I'm sorry.'

She gave him a look that he felt might indicate partial forgiveness yet also a demand for further reparations. He flushed a little, realising he didn't want her to forgive him. He didn't want to return to the somewhat sad world of hers. This was a moment when he could separate himself from her but he couldn't stand to hurt her even for her own good. She could edit her hurt away in a second though, he thought. Now would be a perfectly good time to make a break. I love Karla.

'I'm sorry. There's so much to do with the murders. We're all working so hard.' He sat down on a couch and sank backwards.

She came to him and sat beside him, putting a hand on his thigh. 'I'm sorry. I was being selfish. It's really important that you figure out what's going on. My old fashioned hero.'

Her hand on his thigh was warm and welcome. Suddenly she was moaning in his ear like an engine and he felt impossibly aroused and guilty for taking advantage.

#

Heidi and Dayron sat beside Karla, waiting for Ray to respond to the video call request. When he appeared it looked like he hadn't slept since their last call.

'What did you make of the data, Ray?' Karla had never spoken to him before but his look of exhaustion unnerved her.

'This could take a very long lifetime to figure out. There's so much to think about here. Maybe we should start where I left off with Heidi and Dayron last time. With Sugar.'

'Okay, whatever you think.'

'Well, you were all scared to share his malformed memories so you didn't get the full experience.'

Dayron immediately interjected, 'Because we thought they might do some sort of damage. There's no research, nobody really knows what could happen, do they?'

'Exactly right,' surprise on Ray's face. 'In fact nobody really knows if any editing is safe anyway.'

'What do you mean? How can we not know? We made it safer after editing addiction became a problem.' Karla's face showed her disbelief.

Ray spoke quickly, 'We made an enhanced system but we didn't know it was safer, we just assumed it would be.' He smiled as he drummed a single finger on the desk for emphasis.

Still sporting her look of disbelief, Karla asked why it would have been released at all if that was the case. She thought Ray sounded pleased that he was able to confound her expectations. He said it was untested and nobody at any point had ever claimed otherwise. Somehow people had just ignored the potential danger. And in any case he saw no way to test it without lengthy studies that nobody seemed to have the patience for.

Karla found herself angry, 'So why the fuck do we use it so much?'

Dayron answered, 'Try taking editors away from people and see how happy they are about it.'

'They'd get over it,' Karla dismissed his comment. 'They'd get over it pretty quickly if you told them it could damage them forever.'

Dayron wouldn't concede the point. 'But all you can say is you don't know if it's safe. You don't know it's unsafe.'

'I guess we'll know eventually if it's safe or not,' said Karla. 'Maybe we're finding out right now.'

'Maybe not. We have no control group to compare with.' Heidi was the voice of reason.

'Can we return to the point for a moment please,' said Ray. 'Whether or not you believe, as I do, that editing is damaging to mental health, these malformed memories are in fact dangerous. Furthermore, I believe Sugar to be a sort of prototype for these new monsters you have boxed for interrogation.'

Karla felt a sinking feeling, 'You'd better explain your reasons, Ray.'

'I've done what many scientists have done through the ages when there's no opportunity to perform ethical tests on subjects.'

'You've experimented on yourself, haven't you?' Karla sat back in her seat. 'Are you going to be okay?'

'I can't be sure, honestly.' Karla thought he looked a little sad as he said it. Maybe it was pride or self-pity. 'But I know those memories carry some other sort of information or infection. Now when I use my editor for any purpose those specific memories become powerfully triggered. There's a violent rage in me that wasn't there before. Also a lust.'

'Can't you just erase those memories?'

'I already tried. Unfortunately they've already become like old memories, distributed so widely and so deeply connected to everything else in my life, that removing them would probably require a full wipe.' His voice had become level, losing all the enthusiasm he had seconds ago.

'Ray, this may sound melodramatic but are you a danger to others right now?'

'I honestly don't know the answer to that.'

'Maybe you'd better come here and we can talk and work in person, just in case your condition deteriorates. I'll send somebody to escort you.'

'I'm not going to run away.'

'No, you're not.' Karla heard an edge in her own voice. 'But you can continue your work here under supervision.'

#

Solace woke up to the sound of Ren still sleeping next to him and the first weak glow of sunlight coming through the windows. The weather had changed for the better as summer approached and now there was almost what you might call a proper daytime on Liszt. The light made him optimistic even as sadness for Ren made him reach out and touch her bare shoulder. She made a noise and nuzzled him. She looked so young and soft yet, he remembered, she was an old woman and he an ancient man.

The buzzer sounded, making Ren open her eyes. Solace asked the flat to show the video and Jethro's face appeared on the ceiling above them.

'Jethro! An unexpected pleasure. What time is it? Wait, who cares, just come up.'

'Who's Jethro?'

'A friend I made. We've been to an art class together. We go for drives.'

'When did you find time for that? I thought you were busy on the case?' Ren sat up, awake now.

'Well, a week ago I guess. I don't need to spend every second with Karla and the crew. He's a cool guy, you'll like him.'

There was a knock on the door and Solace shouted to come in, the flat opening the door on his command. Jethro walked into the flat then Solace heard his footsteps approaching their bedroom. He wandered right in and leaned against a wall.

'Still in bed? It's almost summer.'

Solace couldn't help but laugh at him, 'Do you always wander into other people's bedrooms?'

'You said once you thought about my cock. I didn't think you were a prude. Do you want me to give you a minute?'

'You think about his cock?' Ren turned to Jethro, obviously heavily invested in the question.

'I've never even seen his cock,' said Solace, surprised to be having the conversation. Liszt was not a place where you expect to be grilled about your sexual activity.

Jethro, perhaps just for fun, immediately unzipped his one piece suit down past the crotch and revealed his cock and balls, hanging there in the watery orange sunlight.

Ren looked frosty. 'Share.' She said it like a command. Jethro appeared to hesitate with surprise then shrug and they both assumed that somewhat blank expression for a moment. Afterwards Ren leapt to her feet, naked and firm, her labia visible as she climbed over him and headed out of the room past Jethro. Solace had a few seconds of mixed emotions. An intensely sexual urge driven by immediate opportunity, a feeling of freedom, and yet a disturbing feeling of being some sort of abuser.

'She's manipulating you,' whispered Jethro.

'You know your cock is still out?'

'Yes.' He shrugged, put it away.

Solace got out of bed, thinking about a shower and wondering if Ren was going to be annoyed with him. 'I'm going to have a shower,' he walked past Jethro. 'Make yourself at home.' He had no idea why Jethro had come round but he liked the idea of a friend who felt comfortable enough to just drop by. Something he hadn't enjoyed since Karla back on Easy Rider. The memory confused him again as he wandered into the shower where Ren was already standing with her head underwater.

He walked into the shower behind her, putting his hands on her arse cheeks to announce his presence. She didn't react. He moved closer, placing his dick between her cheeks and his hands on her breasts. She didn't stop him but didn't react either, which left him feeling uncomfortable as if he had done something wrong, which indeed he might have. Ren rinsed soap off her body and walked out of the shower. Solace regretted her departure with his dick and felt that guilt again.

When he emerged from the shower, dry, warm and dressed, Solace found Jethro in the lounge listening to music. Ren was nowhere to be seen.

'She left,' said Jethro. 'And you should be glad.'

Solace made no response. He thought about it but couldn't figure out exactly what he felt. Was he happy that she was upset with him and perhaps wouldn't return? He was certainly feeling guilty about fucking her without any desire to continue their relationship. They had never agreed to be monogamous or even discussed it and he felt annoyed that he was expected to ignore other sexual opportunities. She was a sexual animal and enjoyed many partners during her single phases.

'Seriously, she's manipulating you.' Jethro repeated his earlier claim. 'She wants you all to herself. I've shared with her. She couldn't hide it. Quite honestly she scares me a little with her intensity too.'

Solace wondered if Jethro wanted to move their friendship into a sexual relationship but it was too complicated to think about that right now. He wondered, despite his efforts not to, what it would be like to have a threesome with Ren and Jethro. It wouldn't seem right to invite him to participate with Karla. Again his guilt came. 'Do you want something to drink?'

'I was thinking about going for a drive actually.'

'Why not? I'll check to see if I've got any messages from Karla first.'

'Are you working on those murders?' asked Jethro. Solace walked back into the bedroom to fetch his outdoor one piece suit and heard Jethro shout from the other room, 'There's a rumour that you have somebody for them.'

'It's all too complicated and depressing to explain even if I was allowed,' he said as he returned to the room. 'Shall we go?'

The sun was weak and didn't make it feel much warmer but it did change the mood. Solace found it hard to be depressed in sunlight. He could see every smudge and streak on the windscreen reflecting and scattering light before it cleaned itself as they entered the car.

Jethro put on some cello music that filled the car before driving off towards the outer regions of the colony. Solace could occasionally hear the cellist breathing and it annoyed him a little but the playing was so good he ignored it. Now both women were gone from his head as they sped along the streets.

Ten

'Where are you?'

'I'm out by the marshes with Jethro. What's up?'

'What do you do out there?'

Solace didn't want to be asked that. It was hard to define and talking about it could easily destroy the delicate balance between doing something and overthinking things. In the weeks since he and Jethro had met they had come to share the pleasure of being out there in the wilderness of an alien planet. It was something remarkable to savour.

'We're just here. On an alien planet.'

There was a pause before Karla spoke again. Solace wondered if there was a judgement taking place in that short gap. 'I get you. It's quite a big leap from Scotland. I don't want to disturb you, and those contemplative moments are really important, but I just wanted to update you. Can you come by later on today?'

'Of course. I'll see you in a while. Love you.'

There was something different about the landscape in the already fading light. They could see for miles across the gently waving grass in this flat basin. The mist was absent today, Solace realised. To the right there was a distant ghost of a mountain rising up into the enormous blank sky. Solace had never seen it before, having only been there in the dark and swirling mist. He thought the sight deserved some birds circling overhead but Liszt had no native flying creatures. There were not yet any flowers, fruit or insects to sustain them.

'I've only seen the horizon a handful of times before now.'

'Could do with a few trees to break it up,' said Solace.

Jethro glanced at Solace, 'The mist makes everything claustrophobic but when it's gone we find ourselves on an empty world.'

'We could be in an early computer simulation of a world. Maybe under this grass there's a grid pattern on the ground.' Solace thought back to his childhood on Earth when personal computers were a novelty and wireframe graphics were beautiful.

'What's that over there, at the base of the mountain? I thought I saw movement.' Jethro narrowed his eyes.

'Waving grass?' Solace peered into the distance. 'Is there a railway over there? Maybe it was a train.'

'No railway but good thought – perhaps there's a road I don't know about.' He looked over towards their car, barely visible above the grass. The car dutifully released a small drone from some hidden orifice and Solace watched it shoot straight up.

'Are you getting a drone feed? Times like this I wish I had an editor.'

'Yes,' said Jethro, distracted. Solace watched in silence, waiting for news. 'There's a road of sorts. Single lane, winding and kind of overgrown at the edges so probably made in a single pass from a juggernaut years ago.'

'Wonder why it's not on the map. Is there a vehicle on it?'

'Yup. Something coming our way but not particularly quickly. Let me zoom in. Okay, it's definitely not one of the standard cars. It's old and pretty rugged looking. Bit of a beast.'

'Does the road intersect with the one we're on?'

'Looks like the other road ends not far from ours,' said Jethro, still squinting despite seeing the feed in his head. 'You want to go and meet whoever it is?'

'Are you kidding? I'm desperate to know who it is and where they've been.'

'I doubt if it'll be as interesting as you think,' said Jethro as he began to walk back towards the car.

The vehicle was much larger than the car. It had a lot of rugged wheels and what looked like a track that could be lowered to the ground in situations that required more traction. Solace thought it looked like a vehicle designed for exploring other planets ought to look. As he stood next to Jethro the vehicle come to a halt in front of them. A figure stepped out of the cab and onto the footplate. Like most people on Liszt he wore a full bodysuit but his appeared more industrial with none of the usual decorations and some additional loops and pockets bulging with equipment.

The figure appeared to spend a few seconds assessing Jethro and Solace before he jumped down the few feet or so to the ground. He landed with poise and stood facing them as he reached up to undo his hood.

Solace was shocked to see an ancient lined face staring at him. Jethro had opened his hood in greeting and Solace finally remembered to do the same.

'You boys needn't try to share with me, I don't have one of your editors stuffed in my skull.'

'That makes two of us,' said Solace, warming to the man immediately. 'I'm not a big fan of editors and until recently I looked as old as you too.'

'I suppose at some point I'll rewind my face but I feel like hanging on to it for a while yet. Don't let the body degrade in other ways though. I'd be dead in a week on this planet.'

'Are you enjoying the sunshine?' asked Jethro.

'I look old but I'm not your granny, son. Yes, I'm enjoying the fucking sunshine. Are you having a nice day?' The old man loaded his voice with condescension.

'Sorry. I wasn't sure how to initiate a conversation with a stranger who's driving his ancient vehicle to a dead end road in the middle of nowhere,' said Jethro in placid tones.

'Silly boy. I only stopped because you were standing staring at me. This land explorer can tackle almost any terrain. I usually drive straight across this area onto the main road.'

'I've only been awake a short while on this world but I've never seen anybody like you or a vehicle like yours. Where do you go on the main road?'

'Been in stasis have you? Maybe you're still a decent sort then. Why don't you both come in the back there,' he waved one arm at the rear of his vehicle, 'and we can keep warm and have a cup of tea watching the sun go down?'

The three of them sat in the rearmost module of the explorer which was laid out rather like a living room with picture windows on three sides and a transparent roof. Despite it being the old man's natural appearance, Solace thought his wizened face seemed like an affectation when it could have been smooth and youthful instead. He reached for his weak, hot tea served in a dark glass mug. Steam rose off it against an out of focus backdrop of setting sun and endless field of gently waving grass.

'Grass pretty much covers the continent now,' said the old man watching Solace look out the window. 'More and more of the soil is becoming capable of growing things a pioneer might actually eat.' He sat down and raised his mug towards Solace, 'Don't let them give you one of those editors. It'll ruin you.'

'I don't feel ruined,' Jethro said. The old man looked at him and took some tea, nodding. 'Why do you think editors are a bad thing?'

'I used to be one of the people that ran this place, son. I watched people getting hooked on editing, drugs, and hedonism. Selfish, childish people. Tried to fix things but it wasn't to be. Some of us fled that hellhole and built our own places. We're almost certainly doomed though. There are too many of you and your kind and you'll take over the world soon enough and sweep us aside.' He drank more tea as if his fatalistic view was nothing but idle chat.

'How long have you been out there?' asked Solace.

'Forty years, give or take. There are over a hundred of us in a valley beyond the mountains. Many more who ran further to escape your influence. We farm in our own greenhouses and we supplement that with some dried goods I pick up every year from friends that work in your greenhouses. Some of the last sane people in the colony work in those greenhouses. They also give me seedlings of new varieties. Gossip too, I suppose we have to call it. News of the ongoing decline of your society.'

'Meanwhile you deliberately endure hardship as if life only has meaning through hard work and pain?' Jethro challenged him.

'Hardship is to be avoided if possible but not through a distortion of reality. There's no point being freezing cold but feeling warm. No point feeling happy when your lot is miserable and needs improved.'

'So long as you have nothing against pleasure itself then we're in agreement,' said Jethro. 'I don't edit or share any more than is required to get along with people.'

The old man nodded, glancing at Solace. He seemed to be warming to Jethro now, thought Solace. Confirmation of this came when the man spoke again.

'You know there are groups of people hanging around out here on the outskirts? Creepy and up to no good. I avoid them. You have to be careful who you talk to out here.'

Jethro looked at him, perhaps wondering whether to tell his own stories of meeting people out here but remaining silent on the matter. The last of the daylight was reddening behind the mountains, telling of distant lands.

'I wonder if I might come with you?' Jethro's question, uttered flat but somehow charged with emotion, was out of the blue and made Solace feel sad at the thought of losing him.

The man set his cooling tea down and looked at Jethro with something like amused pride and fondness before he glanced back over his shoulder at the mountains. 'You might, son, you might. My name's Fanta.'

#

Yost stood looking down at Yvonne, sleeping soundly below him on the bed. On her forearm where three small cuts arranged neatly side by side. He had anaesthetised her arm to avoid waking her up and being discovered. Then he had cut her for the pleasure of it. He loved her and cried now with the guilt of his actions shuddering through him. Her peaceful face lay innocent and oblivious. A face he had known for longer than most humans had ever lived.

Unable to bear it, he switched off the guilt and his torture ended. He still loved her, obviously. What would she say when she found those cuts? Would she ask him about them or would she realise he must be the culprit and say nothing for fear of what the answer might tell her about him?

He lifted the edge of the covers and looked at her cunt for a few seconds before going for his morning shower.

#

Solace, returned from the outskirts without Jethro for the time being, was on his way up to Karla's apartment. He needed to talk to her quickly if they were to run away with Jethro and Fanta. He had no idea what sort of life to expect but he knew he didn't think much of this one. For the first time he had chosen to run up the stairs rather than take the lift. There was a surprising amount of fun to be had in this fit young body with muscles that never seemed to tire. When he arrived at her door it was already open so he walked straight in and closed it behind him.

'Karla!' he shouted into the flat. 'Where are you?' There was a heavy bouncing noise followed by a medicine ball rolling out of a doorway into the hall in front of him. 'Well that's one way to answer,' he said as he walked towards the room.

The blinds were all open and the lights of the colony blazed in the night. Karla was sitting in the sunken part of her lounge, slumped on cushions. She looked up at him with tearful eyes. 'I can't escape it,' she said. 'I'm so fucking angry that they've taken away my comfort blanket. There's no escape now.'

Undeterred, Solace stepped forward eagerly. He took her by the shoulders and looked her square in the face, 'As a matter of fact I've come to talk to you about an escape.' The excitement was in every part of him and he knew she must be able to detect it but he also knew that where he was concerned this excitement might suddenly fizzle out at any moment. He was just like that. He hoped it would last long enough to influence Karla. 'We met a man travelling beyond the colony. He told us there are habitations beyond the mountains and even people that have wandered farther than that. We don't have to stay here amongst this carnage. Shall we go? Me, you and Jethro?'

The look on her face might have been confusion or shock but Solace took it as a positive if indecisive reaction. 'Now that I can't edit for fear of what might happen to me this place is unbearable. I don't even know if this might be some sort of withdrawal. I feel worse than I've felt for decades. I'm tempted to leave but why would it be any better where this guy lives?'

'They don't edit. They set up their alternative colonies because of what they saw happening here. The guy's like some cool old visionary from the 1960s. He's Dennis Hopper in a space truck, for fuck's sake! And there's nothing to keep us here, is there?'

'What about our friends? What about your little friend Ren? What about the guys on the crew who're fighting the same battles as us? I'm not sure I can abandon them to their fates.' She wiped the almost dry tears from her face.

Solace thought for a moment and realised he did need to say goodbye. In fact he wanted to share with Ren so she could, finally, see his intentions were good and that he had loved her for a while. She could always wipe him from her memory anyway. Probably would. It still mattered to him though. 'Can you activate my editor, Karla? I want to share before I lose it forever. I want to know what it's like in your head. I want to say goodbye to Ren.'

'Now?' she asked. 'You want to edit now when we discover how dangerous it is? That's madness.'

'I've always wanted to share. It sounds amazing and I just want to feel it a few times with a select group of people. Just do it and let's make plans to leave. Please.'

'I don't want to lose you, Solace.' He could see real fear in her face. 'Without my editing refuge you might just be the only thing that makes me feel good.'

'There's always drugs,' he said with a grin.

She pretended to shoot him in the face with her hand, 'You've got 24 hours to edit but I'm setting it to restrict who you can share with. Let's hope it listens to my instructions.'

'I love you.'

'And one more thing. Your first time is going to be with me, not her. Here and now.'

#

Ren had told him to come up, as always. He bounded up the stairs again as he had done just an hour earlier in Karla's building. These thighs are like steel, he thought with admiration. In his mind he had already left her and he assumed she already felt that after their last fractious encounter. So this wasn't a trip to deliver unpleasant news of their breakup but a moment to relish where he was finally able to give her what she had wanted, albeit it a parting gift. Dramatic music played in his head as he walked through her doorway barely out of breath. The theatricality of the moment absorbed him so he didn't want to speak as he saw her walk down the corridor towards him, silhouetted by a warm glow from the living room behind. Her hips swayed as if she was trying to show him what he was missing. She had never looked hotter and he was glad. Rather than waste the surprise he turned sharing on right then without warning.

She obviously wasn't expecting to share with him, believing him incapable, because what he saw was totally unguarded. She realised quickly that he was sharing and seeing her naked mind. She threw up a mask, but it was too late. They both stood still in the dark corridor, looking at each other, knowing.

'Did you become him, Ren? Did you take over where he left off? Or were you always telling that story from the wrong side of the fence? Was it something somebody once said about you?'

She started to walk towards him, saying nothing. Remembering that he had a gun, he pulled it out and pointed it at her. 'Stay where you are. I'm not going to tell on you, don't worry. I'm leaving this place and you with it. I loved you once, you might have seen that. I wanted you to see it. I came here to let you see me.'

'Don't be scared of me, Solace. I'm the same person you always knew. And it's sweet that you came to share with me. I saw you and it was beautiful. I'm glad it didn't end with our last meeting.'

'Loving you is a hazard, Ren. You can't convince me otherwise after what I've just witnessed in your head. I'm like an object to you. We all are. You don't care for me any more than the mountains do. Stay where you are.' He stepped backwards slowly with his gun still at the ready. She reached down and undid her skirt, letting it drop to the floor, then turned and walked away from him. She looked over her shoulder once as she walked into the living room. He watched until her arse vanished from view then he stepped back and closed the door before heading down the stairs, his world view changed.

Eleven

The call from Naz arrived just seconds after Solace had left her with a warm glow. She answered it in a dreamy voice, wondering what role she was playing on this call. She could feel Naz detect her tone but he didn't mention it. Instead he cut straight to the matter at hand. He told her they had boxed an unconnected person who it turned out also shared some of those malformed memories they first found in Sugar. Now she detected a tone in his voice too. Not fear because Naz had a cool head but maybe fatalism. She asked him if that was all, as if it wasn't enough. He said no, there's something else. Yvonne, crying her eyes out and more distraught that anybody had ever known her, said Yost had cut her while she slept. When confronted with the abuse Yost had refused to admit it and shown no remorse.

Karla felt physically unwell as the implications of this knowledge spread through her mind, dark realisations and connections all coming at once like bouts of nausea. Sweat started to pour from her head, sticking her hair to her skull in seconds. She turned the temperature down. Already more pervasive than anybody imagined, more virulent and readily transmitted than expected, and they still had no understanding of how to get rid of it. It might be too late to stop it, she thought. Maybe running is all they could do.

Naz was still on the phone, asking if she was alright, he could see her sweating and looking ill. She told him she was fine. Hesitation revealed his doubts but he asked her what he should do about Yost. Box him and make sure Yvonne has some sympathetic company, she said and ended the call.

Her sweat had dried and she was feeling somewhat better but still light headed. She told the flat to turn the temperature back up to her standard preference, stood up and looked out over the illuminated colony. She called Heidi to find out how it was going with Ray but got no response. She would have to head over there and find out what was going on. Everything felt chaotic and out of control now. She called Solace as she got ready to leave the flat.

'Glad you called actually,' said Solace instead of the usual greeting. 'I got more than I bargained for with Ren.'

'How so?'

'I surprised her with my ability to share and what I saw was frightening. She doesn't care about me at all. Doesn't seem capable of caring.'

'Shit. That must have shocked you.' She paused what she was doing in order to pay full attention to Solace.

'I almost fell on my arse at the shock. Didn't let her see that obviously. We just stood there facing each other, both knowing that I had discovered her. She tried to mask her thoughts somehow. It was like a weird mix of edited in emotions all turned up to the max. I can't describe it very well but she met Jethro and he said her intensity scared him.'

'Oh, where did they meet?'

'Ah, she was at mine and he visited out of the blue.'

'Interesting that he would notice if she's managed to hide it all these years. Maybe he's particularly sensitive to it.' She pulled her jacket over her shoulder as she watched Solace talking, projected on her wall. His face was spread over some blank wall, a doorway, and some pictures. His lips were a metre wide and psychedelic as she watched them move in her still lightheaded state.

'I wonder if she and others like her perpetuate a myth that you can spot a psycho by sharing. It would help them hide more easily. Make you feel safe that they weren't one of the "weird ones" that wouldn't share.'

Karla, dressed and ready, walked out of her flat. 'That would make sense. We're finding out a lot of things we didn't know last week. I feel like we're out of control. I'm just heading in to see what's going on with our technical analysis but it looks increasingly likely that some sort of infection is being passed by sharing certain types of memory.' As she said it she wondered, terrified, if Solace might have been infected by Ren. 'Meet me there and don't share with anybody on the way.'

#

Karla stood in the control room looking at a series of missing feeds. Drones still hovered across the colony wherever she instructed them but half of the crew feeds were absent. Naz had told her as soon as she arrived that things were getting a little messy but the missing crew were frightening. These were friends a few days ago. Yost and Yvonne both gone. Reuben nowhere to be found. Many others too had simply discarded their bracelets and disappeared from the network.

'Naz,' she felt calm and strong as she took command, 'you know they didn't just disappear? Our friends have become casualties of this situation. We have to face the fact that this is more than a mess. This threatens the existence of the whole colony.'

'I know.'

Karla could sense something in his tone, some resentment perhaps. 'You don't seem totally onside here, Naz. Anything up?'

'You were looking and sounding disengaged earlier. I wasn't sure if you were still with us yourself. And in fact it's hard to know, isn't it?'

'Yes, I suppose it's hard to be certain. We can't even share with those we suspect in case we become infected ourselves.'

'This could be spreading catastrophically fast and we have no way of knowing. We're completely powerless. We don't even have somewhere to hide.'

His comments made her ashamed for having broken down at such a critical time. She hoped Solace would arrive safely soon but consoled herself with the idea that they were not at the stage of fighting in the streets and he was armed anyway.

'Let's go downstairs and visit Heidi and Dayron.' She called

Heidi to let her know they were on their way. They had Ray with them now and perhaps they would have some way to develop a solution.

'Guys, I know you always work quickly but we have a new reason for urgency.'

'Quickly? Constantly at full speed with occasional breaks for food, sex, and a five minute snooze.' Dayron looked tired enough for this to be true.

'I know, believe me, I know. But the situation is that several crew have stopped reporting to work, presumed infected with whatever we're dealing with here. Up until now we haven't seen either a public acknowledgement of this condition but by not appearing for work they're telling us they don't feel the need to hide.' She paused and looked around at Heidi, Dayron and Naz. 'I think our discovery of the Virgin Club has caused them to enter a new mode. They've suddenly gone from secretive underground club to people out to spread this condition.'

'Shouldn't we warn people with a public announcement?' asked Heidi, looking uncertain of herself.

'Yes but what do we tell them?' Karla knew there she had to do something but she didn't want to cause a mass panic unless she was certain.

'Turn off sharing immediately and leave it off until further notice?' suggested Dayron.

'And if we don't reach everybody at the same time with that message then the infected are likely to broadcast those malformed memories to everybody in the colony, trying to infect as many as possible before the option disappears.' Karla was wary of anything that might spook the Virgin Club into even more aggressive action. 'It would be good if we had a method of detecting the infected or some way to turn off everybody's sharing rights. Or even a cure. But that's why we're here, to find out what progress there is on the technical front.'

'Okay,' Heidi began, 'the first thing to remember is that we don't know if the crew were infected already or whether it just happened. Of course the latter is more worrying because it implies a rapid expansion. I can tell you from working with Ray that if you are susceptible, then it's easy to become infected by sharing those malformed memories that were buried in Sugar. However it's not so easy to put somebody to sleep and adapt their editor as we've seen in the other cases. There was no opportunity for Yost to be adapted, for example.

'The bad news is that we think those adaptations are there purely for the control of the individual. In other words people will be infected without those adaptations but they won't become some controllable asset. We've seen this with poor Ray.'

'Where is Ray?' asked Karla. 'Is his condition the same?'

'He's boxed and still relatively co-operative. He knows we're trying to help him.' Heidi looked resigned, as if she herself were in the box. 'Dayron, why don't you go and check on him?'

Dayron wandered out, looking tired.

'And can we help him?'

'No, not without wiping most of his memory which realistically means the end of him as the man he was.'

'So we have no cure.' Karla hadn't expected there to be one but it was depressing to hear it said. She tried not to show it on her face. 'But can we think of a way for people out there to identify and avoid those carrying the memories?'

'Even some of the people carrying them don't know about it. Maybe most of them.'

#

Dayron walked into the lab where Ray was in his box. Unlike the prisoners, Ray wasn't kept in a dark box so Dayron caught his eye as he approached.

'Are you okay in there, Ray? Anything you need?'

'Can you bring me a woman? That's my last request.'

'Gallows humour still operational I see.'

Ray banged his head backwards against the padded interior of the box. He looked frustrated and anxious. Of course there was nothing he could do about that in the box, not even edit the emotion out. Dayron felt guilty.

'Karla's here. Asking if there's anything we can do to help you.'

'We both know there's only a full wipe left to try. Waiting is just torture.'

'Maybe we'll come up with a last minute solution. Anyway, you're not the same person from one moment to the next. Identity is a moving target. These days we edit our own life into a movie, separating out emotions we don't like, painting pictures of ourselves. Wiping is just like a reboot really.'

'I thought I was the mental one. This isn't the wipe of one bad memory as you well know. I'm not forgetting an unpleasant year of my life but losing almost every single experience since inception. There will be no me left to rebuild my next iteration. It's one tiny step short of killing.'

'Sorry. I'm not particularly good at this comforting people business.'

'I used to love talking to people like you but now it's a bit of a chore. Sorry. No time left to be nice. And anyway, since I genuinely feel a desire to cut people into pieces I'm not sure adding rudeness to my list of faults makes any material difference.'

'What's it like when you think about killing?' Dayron stepped closer to the box, unperturbed by Ray's comments.

'Like sexual desire mixed with addiction and the thrill of doing something illicit. It's almost irresistible.'

'I think I'll go back and see what's happening with the others.'

#

'How is he?'

'Beyond repair, I think,' said Dayron. 'At least he knows his fate though.'

They stood around the large room, distributed randomly at desks, leaning on walls and staring at screens. Karla paced a little while the others watched her, apparently waiting for her instructions. While she was deep in thought one of the screens caught everybody's attention. The Plaza at Shelter, seen from a hovering drone, tiny figures limned with yellow outlines by the targeting system were running after a single figure. It was some sort of chase. Naz changed a few settings and other screen provided different views of the same scene. A fleeing woman's terrified face chilled them all as it raced past their vantage point in silence.

'Volume,' said Karla to her bracelet and they heard a cacophony until she pointed at the screen to focus. A hubbub of exclamations and shouts filled the room, the woman's screams fleeing with her.

'Who do we have nearby to assist?' Karla couldn't take her eyes off the screens as the woman managed to maintain a gap between her and the pursuers.

'Nobody who's responding, and these guys on screen have bracelets but no ID' said Naz, looking at Karla with shock on his face. She turned away from the screen at his announcement.

'If I was being chased in such a crowded place I would share my distress and ask for assistance,' Karla spoke as if asking herself a question out loud. They were all staring at the screens as the familiar face of Yost briefly filled the frame. The drone had flown by him, tracking one of the runners, and had accidentally captured his hunter's look in passing. 'Track back on Yost, two drones. What's he looking at?'

One of the screens showed a sweeping view as a drone circled back behind Yost and lined up over his shoulder. It was a tiny drone and he wouldn't even be aware of its presence unless he was sharing the feeds.

'Feeds private to this room,' Karla gave the instruction, aware that crew facilities might be used to track and hunt people. This turn of events was unexpectedly swift.

The view over Yost's shoulder was a shot through the crowds. A tunnel of bodies at the end of which stood an attractive woman staring open-mouthed after the fleeing woman. She turned this way and that, as if looking for assistance before finally catching sight of Yost staring at her. As fear appeared on her face the other drone, now arriving behind her, swung round to reveal the cruelty on Yost's face. There was a gasp in the room.

'He's not part of some organised group but he's a dangerous lone hunter. There's no telling how many others have been infected by the same memories but judging by the pace of change in Yost and Ray I'd have to guess that most of the colony could become a rabid killer inside a week. There's just no way to stop this, is there?' Karla turned to Heidi, Dayron and the others. She wasn't so much looking for an answer as confirmation that she was right in her assertion that it was hopeless. 'We can't stop this,' she said.

'They've stopped chasing that poor woman,' Heidi had been following the chase.

She was right. All of those yellow outlines were now static and flashing slowly to indicate they were still targeted. The ones still on the edge of the plaza started to trickle out towards the others in the streets beyond and then fan out to either side. Karla and Naz set a series of drone sweeps to survey the area. Everybody was fixed to the screens as one drone caught up with the fleeing woman. For a second her breathing and scared little noises filled the room, larger than life as the drone danced unnoticed a foot from her head. It saw down the streets she passed and in one of them to her left it caught another figure walking towards Shelter Plaza. The figure, looking startled by the woman's flight, glanced in her direction. His hood was up but his eyes and stance told Karla immediately that it was Solace.

'Solace! Shit! He's coming back from Ren's flat to Shelter. He's making his way here.' She was already calling him while Naz told a drone to approach him.

An elevated view showed the streets like a map, the yellow outlined figures making for all the intersections, all the roads Solace might turn down. It was the strategy you might deploy if you wanted to catch Solace in a slowly closing net. The width of their blockade was increasing so that he would not be able to get around them.

Karla watched the figure on the screen raise his phone, saw her own holographic head looking at him. 'Solace, you're being hunted right now. Stop and retreat immediately. I'm watching on drone, I'll guide you.'

'Who's hunting me?' He had already turned around and headed back towards the outskirts.

'I don't know but they're organised which makes me think they're connected to the murderers calling themselves the Virgin Club. I don't know why they would target you though, unless they're after anybody connected with authority. Duck into the next left and as soon as you're round the corner sprint to the next junction.' She wanted to put some distance between him and the pursuers before they knew he had spotted them.

'It sounds like things have moved on since we last spoke,' Solace sounded calm and effortless. 'I'm glad you gave me a gun.

How many bullets does it have and how many men are following me?'

'Bullets are tiny so you have thousands of them, don't worry about that. I don't know if the men are armed but there are nine of them heading towards you. Okay, as you approach this corner stop running and walk diagonally to the next intersection.' It was difficult to gage visibility for the men three streets back. The mist and light sleet might make Solace invisible to them at this distance.

'Is there a plan here? Nine men seems like quite a few and didn't the guys you captured before have their own drones?'

'Heidi, Dayron and Naz are all piloting drones armed with pacifiers as we speak. We should be able to get there and take them down so I just need you to keep a good distance. And yes they did have some drones at their meeting but not many and I haven't seen any in operation today either.'

'I thought they were tiny anyway?'

'Eyes are tiny, pacifiers are big enough to shoot down if you see one.'

'You're assuming I'm a good shot!' Solace was still breathing smoothly as if his effort was minimal, which was a comfort to Karla.

Naz, blank faced from concentration on his drone feed, spoke to Karla without looking at her. 'I'm coming up on the rearmost targets. I just wondered about the bigger picture. It seems to me that these issues are already too big for us to handle.'

'You mean what's our exit strategy? I've been thinking about it myself. We need to take down as many of these guys as we can then get in cars and pick Solace up. We all need to be armed and we might not be coming back here anytime soon.'

'But where is there to go?'

'We're going to the colony on the other side of the mountain,' she said as if it had been her plan for some time rather than a last resort only just arrived at. Some surprise crept onto the faces of all listening but nothing more was said as their pacifier drones now approached targets.

Karla watched the screens as the others piloted their drones behind the targets. They had all converged on one group in order to take the targets down simultaneously in the hope that the alarm wouldn't be raised. Three shots took the two targets down silently and Karla watched the screens for any sign of alarm. It had been a perfect take down but all of the other targets stopped moving simultaneously.

'Shit, they're in continuous contact with each other. They must be using their editors as relays to share at this distance. They're part of some kind of network and each of them is a node.' She went to the highest drone for the widest view, now concerned about how many others might be part of the network. The intelligent targeting system showed dozens more yellow pixels converging towards Solace from much further away, some of them obviously coming out of their houses. The alarm must have been raised. 'We're fucked now. There are too many of them. Guys, take down the targets nearest to Solace, no stealth required but don't get shot down. Solace, you need to head out of town as quickly as you can and we'll be coming to get you soon. Just go straight out towards the burbs.'

Although the pacifiers were fast and hard to hit, when they caught up with the killers their pilots found the enemy had unexpected long range accuracy. They must be using intelligent munitions of some sort. The pacifiers only had an effective range of about 25 metres and it was tough to get that close. Naz had arranged for reserve pacifiers to follow them, awaiting their human pilots before being allowed to fire on human targets, and they took these over as their own drones were shot down. Karla began to wonder how long they ought to remain here given that this was turning into a battle they couldn't win.

'Guys, keep flying but I'm going to guide us all out of the building into a couple of cars. Solace, we've taken out eight of the nine that were chasing you but now we have a whole host of other targets and the bastards keep shooting down our drones. We'll run out of drones long before we get you to safety so we're coming after you now.'

'I keep catching a glimpse of him through the sleet. It's heavier now and visibility's crap but at least I know it's just one man. What about all the other people in Liszt though – what's happening?'

'As soon as we get in a car I'm going to broadcast a message to everybody. Things have fallen apart so quickly though, I don't know that anything will make any difference now.' She was already dragging the others after her, their attention almost entirely on their drones and the battle outside. 'I won't be much help to you for a little while, Solace, but I'm coming for you.'

'I love you, Karla.'

'I love you too,' and it was true.

She led the team down into the garage under Shelter. A sense of urgency was upon them and they ran through the underground space towards the exit. Karla had already called one of the identical cars with another slaved to it that would follow them on their journey until needed. She could hear it approaching from behind them, tires squealing on the smooth floor. The first car came to a halt beside them and they all got in.

As soon as they were in the car Karla called Jethro.

'Jethro. This is Karla. Solace might have mentioned me.'

'Karla. Yes, I know your name.'

'Good, listen. Solace is in trouble and I'm on my way to help him but we need to rendezvous with you as soon as possible after that. Are you ready?'

'Yes,' said Jethro.

Good boy, don't ask questions, thought Karla, glad of his trust in her. She had already hung up. The car was finally at the exit which opened automatically as they climbed its slope, revealing a rectangle of dark sky and thick sleet blustering through their headlights.

With the car on its way to Solace and Jethro warned this was her first opportunity to think about the ramifications of her departure. She had to prepare a message to send out to the hapless inhabitants of Liszt for whom salvation looked impossible. She worried that she might be missing a possible solution; that she was leaving them all behind to be slaughtered. There were virtually no crew left and her superiors had inexplicably ignored her since they had caught their first killer. She could think of no safe place to be inside this colony. All she could do was warn people and hope that the murderers were not so numerous that they could not be overpowered.

She sent out the message on general broadcast as a public service announcement. She attached several files to it with details but the headline news was succinct.

You may not believe this at first but pay careful attention then view the attached files for confirmation. Sharing could expose you to a dangerous viral memory that turns you into a killer. There is no way to tell whether or not somebody is infected. It can happen to anybody and appears to transform them within a day, maybe quicker or slower depending on the individual. Some of the killers are acting as an organised group but those infected now merely turn into killers with their own desires and agenda. Nobody knows exactly how this started but we know editing causes some form of damage, particularly with repeated heavy use. I advise you to cease using your editor.

We don't know how to stop this infection short of a full wipe. Gangs of killers are on the rampage across the colony right now. Arm yourself and stay close to those who you trust. Colony representatives and leaders appear to be involved. Crew are not responding to requests for assistance so consider them compromised as well. Turn off sharing now. Accept no broadcasts after this. Be suspicious of those who attempt it.

We continue to fight those we can but there are too many of them. We have no idea how many are infected.

Attached files:

Video of interviews and forced sharing with subjects.

Video of the capture of 27 killers calling themselves the Virgin Club.

Video of interview with a researcher who experimented on himself.

The cars powered through the network of lower level spirals heading up towards ground level.

\#

Solace had been on the run for a good ten minutes and was finally getting fatigued with running through the slippy streets. He was sick of the continuous sleet that made progress so difficult but at the same time thankful that the killer on his trail couldn't see him clearly. He looked back and saw nothing. He knew if he waited a few seconds he would see the relentless figure coming out of the curtain of sleet like a shadow. It was beautiful to watch, he thought despite the danger. Even the buildings beside him disappeared from sight at impossibly low heights. Perhaps he could hide but Karla told him to keep running to the burbs.

Now the killer behind him appeared; just a moving darkness going in and out of visibility across one single street, catching sight of Solace and raising an arm now. Solace ducked and moved behind a wall in time to evade whatever munition bit into the wall with a noise, almost lost in the sleet, like somebody spitting a seed out of their mouth. It should have made a more frightening noise, he thought. He looked round the corner again to see the killer half way across the street with his arm still raised and retreated immediately. Another bullet chewed another bit of the wall in front of him.

Is this really a man that I'm facing, thought Solace. He's a relentless machine of a man at best. His head full of murder, repeated over and over. Repetition that forces all other thoughts out of his head. One word repeated in a driving rhythm. Hunt. Instruction one of a set: await confirmation of task before moving on to the next. Predecessor complete. Target acquired. Kill. When they hunted women he was one of a group of people working in concert. Each of them doing one part only. This guy is the killer today but maybe the butcher tomorrow. Maybe the hunter another day. Venerable art critic the next. Just an organ of a bigger body.

Solace rolled sideways from behind the building, firing his gun in blind hope until he was able to target the killer. No need. His first shot had been lucky and the man who was a few short steps from the corner was already falling into the deep sleet on the pavement. His head cracked with a disgusting noise as his forehead made contact. Solace winced and almost threw up. Instead he forced himself to stand up and inspect the fallen man. Blood was mingling with the sleet but he wasn't sure he was dead. Rather than inspect him more closely he picked up the man's gun, put it in his pocket and walked onwards towards the burbs. He broke into an easy jog that he could maintain for as long as required and wondered how many more assailants might come after him.

His phone rang as he ran. It was Karla, at last.

'Coming up behind you Solace. There are two cars, get in the second one.'

'Thank fuck.'

The cars sprayed sleet everywhere but Solace didn't care. He stepped into the second car and found it empty but at least it was warm as the doors closed behind him. The car moved off again immediately.

'Sorry, this car's full already but at least we can talk through the car and not that old phone.'

'We could have shared too, since you turned on my editor.'

'What a time to turn on his editor,' said Naz quietly without losing focus on his drone feed.

'Definitely don't do that,' warned Karla. 'As soon as I sent out my public service announcement we started getting spammed by share requests from people in every building nearby. I think they're trying to spread the virus to anybody and everybody now the truth is public. And our drones are showing increased activity all over the colony.'

'It's beyond our ability to deal with it,' said Naz. 'All we can do is keep clearing a path for ourselves as we go.'

'Who else is with you in that car?'

'Heidi and Dayron. They can't speak right now as they're not used to controlling drones in combat, although obviously they've had the training. We're on our way to Jethro. I wasn't able to give him the full story but you can call him now if you like. We should be there in about ten minutes.'

#

'What was that about?' asked Fanta as he and Jethro wandered down the aisles.

The smell of the plants was more evocative even than the sight of them all in one place or the sensation of brushing past leaves. Dust had gathered in corners and under the plant beds where it would occasionally drift across the smooth floor when a nearby door was opened or closed. Jethro listened intently to their footsteps which evoked images of empty cathedrals back on Earth, nobody left to walk their halls. He closed his eyes and there was jungle echoing under the dome. 'We really do need birds,' Jethro stopped to listen to all the little noises of watering systems, pumps, vapour that misted onto the leaves nearby. 'I'm afraid we're going to have to leave in a hurry, Fanta.' He opened his eyes and looked at the man beside him. 'I'm not sure what's happening but I think we're about to be visited by a horde of murderers.'

'That's some assertion for somebody who doesn't know much but I'll take you at your word. You'll have to leave that bracelet behind.'

'Of course. But for now it guides my friends to us. Maybe we should head back to your explorer and be ready to leave?'

'We're stocked up and ready to go. I don't think your cars are equipped to follow us and we only have room for ten passengers. Just thought I should mention that in case you're planning a mass exodus.'

'You don't seem worried by the hordes of murderers.'

'They've been here for a long time, son. Nothing particularly new to worry about.' Fanta led the way back to his vehicle that sat, massive, on the road outside the greenhouse. 'We'll head back to the marsh and they can meet us there. They move rather faster than us anyway.'

Jethro followed him, thinking about Fanta's comment, wondering how he could be so confident about it. 'Fanta,' he caught up and looked him in the face, 'what exactly makes you say they've been here for a long time?'

'Oh, just that we left for exactly that reason decades ago.' He carried on walking.

'You know who and what they are, don't you?'

Fanta sighed in a tired way, nodded, 'Yes, yes I do.'

Twelve

Solace wondered if he was in quarantine, back here in the slave car. But no, Karla wouldn't have brought him along if he was under suspicion, despite her affection for him. She had actually uttered the words studiously avoided in the past. Now they were past the time for caution and she had done her own equivalent of throwing herself on his mercy. Everything inside the car was beautiful and well made, he noticed again. He took pleasure in the comfort of the seat as he watched the aerial view of their location, their cars two targeted dots moving through the outer reaches of habitation. As far as he could make out they were not being followed. The original assailants were all down and those that had given chase after that appeared to have lost interest as the cars got farther from the centre of the colony.

He wondered why they might have given up the chase, finally, after such a battle. *Because they can sense that I'm infected? Might I be?* The possibility scared Solace even though he felt no different than before. *I feel no guilt over the killing of the man who followed me.* But he had nothing to compare it to, having never killed a man before. Does it even make sense to talk of a normal reaction to killing somebody when it's such an extreme act, he wondered. *I took no pleasure in it. Not even satisfaction. Just disgust at the blood and the thought of death, the extinction of a person.*

'Solace.' Karla's voice cut through the silence between the cars. 'Yes?'

'I didn't put you in the other car as a quarantine measure, in case you were wondering.'

Solace laughed, 'How the hell did you know I was worrying about that?'

'It's the sort of thing you would worry about.'

'So you don't think I'm infected?'

'No, something tells me Ren was a natural born psycho, not somebody infected with this thing.'

They were arriving at the location where the roads were close to each other and the aerial view revealed Fanta's vehicle sitting waiting for them. Two dots emerged from it as the cars slowed to a halt beside them.

Solace saw Jethro and Fanta walking towards the cars slowly, relaxed. He sealed his outer layer and opened the door on a harsh cold although the sleet had stopped or at least wasn't falling here. He had a feeling that something of significance was happening here and started to notice the details about the world around him and his own body as if they were suddenly very important. He watched his feet step onto the ground and listened to noise of slush being compressed and displaced, had a sudden longing for the crisp sound of thick snow instead.

Karla was already out of her car and walking towards Fanta. She said something he couldn't hear over the thin wind that swept their words away, undulating with the grass towards the distant mountains. He almost didn't want to hear words that might disrupt this surreal feeling that things were happening around him without his influence. He couldn't decide if it was a comforting lack of control or a disturbing sense of being disembodied.

He walked closer until he could hear them talking. They were talking about leaving the cars behind and going in Fanta's explorer. It was important but not urgent to leave soon. The others milled around listening but not interrupting. Jethro nodded at Solace, some sort of look on his face. I'll sleepwalk into whatever this is, thought Solace. Fanta waved towards his vehicle and everybody looked at everybody else as if to confirm their presence before departure. Solace was last to walk up the steps and knew he would soon have to start giving the world his full attention again. At the top of the steps Karla stood smiling down at him, already taking off her outdoor gear.

The explorer made its way across the landscape autonomously, wheels bumping across the terrain while the modules on top remained almost perfectly flat. The lights were on inside and out. Solace and the others sat in the rear, some of them watching the explorer looking like a toy on screen as seen by the drones following overhead. Solace looked out the window at the passing scenery and remembered being on a train in Scotland at the end of some anonymous winter day. His reflection in the window looked like a man recovering from exercise with hair stuck to his head in places, flushed patches on his face. Remnants of his long chase through the sleet. He leaned his forehead on the cold window and looked into his own pale blue eyes.

Jethro, reflected in the window, was delivering cups of tea to the newly arrived members of the group. Solace felt Jethro's hand on his shoulder briefly, reassuring. The others were obviously interpreting his withdrawal as a reaction to the day's events and no doubt they were right. He was glad they had given him the space.

'Are we being followed?' Karla turned to Fanta who was arriving in the module.

Fanta asked the explorer to show drone two and the screen displayed about a mile of territory around the explorer. From the high viewpoint all they could see was a tiny glint of light from their headlights moving slowly through the darkness. Up ahead there were some white clouds and mist that they would soon enter as they journeyed towards the mountains. 'They're unlikely to follow. I've never seen them this far from the colony before.'

'You keep talking about them as if they're a familiar adversary. What do you know, Fanta?' As Jethro said it the others turned to Fanta as if now realising there had been a previous conversation on the topic.

'I'm afraid I'm to blame,' Fanta looked older than ever. Solace watched the others react to him with fear, maybe wondering what he was hiding behind his ancient flesh. 'I used to be one of the colony leaders – way back on Easy Rider, before we even got to Liszt. We tried to stop the rot of selfish hedonism we thought would destroy our colony before it even started. We were arrogant, stupid and desperate.' Fanta looked around as if asking for questions but nobody spoke and he continued. 'People struggled with long lives. Relationships, boredom, depression. Editing made everything unreal. People didn't have to care so much about each other. Compassion and empathy became choices. Unpopular ones too. People just refused to take personal responsibility for anything. Despite our long lives we had started behaving as if only the moment mattered. Consciousness was like a searchlight of poignancy passing through an uncaring universe.

'If technology had changed us then perhaps it could be manipulated to change us in better ways, we thought. And why not?' He looked around the module at attentive faces.

'What exactly did you do?' Solace was becoming animated again as Fanta's story dragged him back to the world. His question carried no menace or judgement.

'We were interested in consciousness, personal identity and collaborative behaviour. Ever since I read The Selfish Gene in my teenage years on Earth I was looking for a way to show that animals evolved in at the group level. I saw an opportunity with the new editors to play with that. Long before you had the ability to share through your editors we had developed prototypes. We worked out a way to share thoughts in the hope that a consciousness might develop at a meta level and in some way influence our behaviour to be less selfish and more altruistic towards other people in the group.'

The group listened in silence, rapt. Solace watched the hairs on the back of his veined hand stand a little erect, felt a tension in his body. He could see where this was going.

'We wanted to bring unity and stability for the long term cohesion of society. We knew being colonists was going to be tough and the way things were going it was already looking like a disaster. We might have been the only ship to make landfall and build a successful colony. The human race might have depended entirely on our success. Failure was an extinction event for humanity.' Fanta spoke a little more quickly, raised his youthful hands and arms like an appeal for reason and understanding of their position.

'How does it work? Like our own consciousness – a monitoring system of our other mental systems? Some form of oversight?'

Solace was still interested in the mechanisms, somehow not fazed by the revelations.

'Pretty much. Networks of thoughts passing through connected editors, aware of the thoughts in each unit…'

'Units?' Karla laughed and looked at Fanta with incredulity.

'…creating a sort of consciousness we think.'

'You're not even sure? Fantastic work.' Karla looked angrier than the others who were perhaps still in shock.

Solace still wanted more detail and tried to keep their enquiries calm. 'How would it be possible to tell if it was conscious or not? Is there some way to listen in like we do to each other?'

Fanta looked at him with narrowed eyes, 'Yes, you're spot on. We gathered that data easily enough – interpreting it is another matter. What language would an artificial meta intelligence speak? What would it think about? Some of us are still trying to work on that but we have a very small team and it's difficult work.' He looked down at his tea and sat back in his seat as if ready now for more questions.

'Just in case there's any doubt left, can I just clarify this: the murderers are part of this kind of hive mind construct?' Karla was leaning forward into the circle of people, intent.

'It started decades ago but went undetected. Some of our experimental subjects became victims of abuse at the hands of the sort of people we were trying to change. The connections were made, shared and spread throughout the population like a poison. Too deep and too widespread for us to excise it. By the time we understood it was way too late.'

'And that's when you left the rest of us to our fate without even a warning.' Karla's anger was barely controlled.

'We think there might be a collection of memes that, when all are present in a single individual, allow for the emergence of a set of behaviours. A very specific character that is probably based on those original experiences back on the ship. It wasn't safe for us to remain there and challenge that – you've seen that it hunts its enemies. We had to retreat and search for solutions. We're still doing it. Still trying to salvage something if we can. It's going to be much harder now that the entity is discovered. We can't predict what it will do now.'

They might all have felt the same thing, sitting there in the explorer as it drove them through the Liszt night towards a sanctuary beyond the mountains. Their friends and families were behind them now trapped in the midst of a malevolent colony with barbaric desires and unknown purpose.

#

The night was almost over by the time the explorer reached the foothills and there was a glow seeping upwards from the horizon. Solace didn't see who woke up first but they were all awake now and looking at the screens.

'Still nobody following. Maybe they won't bother.' Heidi sat cross legged beside Dayron. They had both been silent last night during Fanta's confession, or explanation perhaps, it being difficult to assess exactly how he viewed himself and his fellow experimenters. Both Heidi and Dayron seemed the type to gather data ravenously before coming to conclusions.

'Busy murdering each other,' Dayron mumbled as he lounged next to Heidi, drawing dark looks from Karla and Naz.

The screens showed uninterrupted plains of grass growing against all the odds in the frozen marshes. Potential routes between the mountains could be seen just ahead. Behind them nothing moved.

'He's right you know. They have no desire to chase us. They have what they want and they know we can't stop them.' Fanta leaned against the entrance to the module having come from the cab where he had slept in the reclining driver's seat. 'They've never come after me in all the years I've been visiting the greenhouses.'

Fanta had a kind of authority when he spoke, Solace thought. It could have been his ancient face or just the fact that they were in his vehicle heading for his colony. He felt the explorer begin to ascend into the foothills.

Thirteen

The colony beyond the mountains was a shock to the new arrivals. Compared to the city they had just left behind this was a tiny village. A flat plain at the bottom of a valley stretched for miles into the distance whilst the sides rose steeply into flat topped mountains. A collection of habitation modules rose out of a ground level mist that was the only soft edge to be seen. It was early and white light turned grey as it emerged from the habs and guttered just a few metres from the windows. It reminded Solace of bad film sets from 1960s science fiction.

Several doors opened and people came forward and surrounded the explorer which had just rolled to a stop. Fanta was already on his way out of the explorer to meet them as Solace made his way to the front of the vehicle. The light from the explorer illuminated young faces, leaving Solace wondering about Fanta's choice not to roll back his own face. Whatever the people at the bottom of the steps were talking to Fanta about didn't sound like a friendly greeting. There was distress in their voices.

'They've sent signals to all the other ships and colonies. That was all she said then the signal stopped. No idea if she was caught or if she's okay.'

Solace exited the explorer and apart from a vague nod from one of the men standing on the fringes of the discussion nobody bothered to acknowledge him.

'So we've no idea about the content of those messages?' Fanta asked the tall man who had delivered the news.

'No. And we've lost almost all of our people, or at least we can't raise them.'

'Who's left?'

'Only Natsuki. She only checked in once yesterday to say she was lying low and not to expect contact for a while. She could be dead, infected or safe. We don't dare contact her for fear of giving her away.'

Solace recognised the name from Karla's team, 'Is she crew?'

The tall man turned to him, obviously already aware of who he was, and replied 'Yes but her primary allegiance is to us. Can you tell us anything useful?'

'Probably not. I just knew the name from Karla's team.' He felt ridiculous trying to add anything given how little he knew about the whole situation.

'Whatever they're up to, we have to assume they've increased their risk appetite now that most of their own citizens are aware of them. They'll seek to maximise their control in as short a time as possible. That probably includes any influence they seek on the other ships, on other planets and colonies.' Fanta spoke with confidence like the leader of a tribe about to go to war. 'If we don't figure out a way to stop them they'll spread this thing to every last person.' He gestured towards the explorer behind him, 'I have a couple of technicians with me here who will bring new ideas to our technical team. We need to take every resource we have and apply it now because there is no time left. Let's meet in an hour and figure out the best course of action.'

Solace looked around at the weathered vehicles, the battered habitats, the hard faces with a fragile resolve. He could see Karla making her way down the corridor of the explorer towards the exit, her handsome face looking out at him. He wanted to know everything that had happened in her life since she put him to sleep on Easy Rider.

#

#

#

End notes

I'm including an old short story here because it was the origin of the character Solace. The story itself has no connection with the novella you've just read but characters often form in my head and end up in different stories. Sometimes people ask me if characters wouldn't be better left in their own universe rather than hopping from one to another. But there's a lot of fun to be had putting people in another universe and asking how their lives might pan out there. Well, it's fun for me anyway.

Moment by Moment

First published in 2015

Here I stand, Solace Bathgate, tall and gentle on the ice. In this bleak and suggestive space thousands of the dead hover beneath us in a crystalline pattern. The clarity of the ice and the winter sun combine to afford us this vertiginous view of the deep. A noise shoots through the ice. I turn to find Dan trembling at the sound.

'Dan. It's frozen solid all the way to the bottom. You can't fall in.' He's an idiot. The others look on, unsurprised.

More than thirty years ago I would desperately try to avoid sharing the exact moment I woke up with millions of others by setting my alarm for odd times. One day it might be 6.34, the next 7.09. I didn't want to be the same as everybody else. Now, here are thousands who chose to die together at the same time, sharing their grief in what I assume was an effort to transform it into something noble.

Yost, whose nose I admire for its mountainous profile, wonders out loud. 'How did they distribute themselves at different depths? Did this entire body of water freeze at the same time?'

'Perhaps they had different degrees of buoyancy. Maybe they all floated but tied themselves at different depths with thin wires or strings we can't see. Whatever it was, they made quite an effort to create this scene.'

A thin mist circulates a few centimetres above the ice, snaking around our ankles in the thankfully light wind. No doubt it accumulated due to the steep hills on each side of this frozen lake. The hills are covered with short dark green trees all the way to the top, the white sky flat behind. I am disturbed by the landscape although I see the beauty in it.

It is almost completely silent now. Even careful footsteps across the ice have ceased, all eyes searching below. People just like them forever suffering a fate they themselves fear.

'Let's get moving again before our feet freeze.' I'm an unlikely leader but right now I know the mood has deteriorated and we need to change the scenery.

#

Thirty years ago my narcissistic clients talked incessantly about themselves and called it *information*. No. Information is when you see a small story on the internet about some weird microbe causing havoc with the ecosystem in Indonesia. Information is important.

Before long we learned that the microbe was just one in a chain of different microbes working like a production line. It was odd to discover these biological factories out of the blue, astonishing to find their DNA was different to anything else ever seen on our planet. The world was rocked not by the question of whether they were of alien origin or home grown artificial life forms, but by the realisation that these voracious microbes might change our world before we could do anything about it. Soon other miniature invaders were discovered smuggling their exobiology into our ecosystem.

It was all explained to us in serious tones by men in suits: 'These hyper efficient organisms evolve faster than us and spread like wildfire so we have to adapt to the new environment rather than try to eliminate the invaders.' They planned to engineer the next humans but nothing could be done to ensure the rest of us remained viable in the new world.

It was with horror that I and billions of others realised our golden years were already behind us. We faced extinction. Life, viewed in its entirety, had become worthless. Now I see it like mathematical integration; if I stack every insignificant slice of time on top of the next I will make them amount to something.

Millions of others chose to make their own exit from this life. It started with bleak private moments but became infectious as stories spread. It was a movement, a comfort, and later a cult. Some made it an art form. Their last act a creative destruction like our brothers and sisters in the ice.

The new humans were issued and, although initially small in number, these children represented our future. But they were clever, strong and agile beyond their years and people who had just spawned normal children feared their progeny would become second class citizens. We remembered the fate of the poor Neanderthals.

But we are worse off, our genes incompatible with the new humans.

We're heading south to warmer climes and from the top of the hill I can see the valley where we'll pitch our tents tonight. The short trees with their bulbous little waxy leaves, their purple underside like heather from a distance, carpet the land in all directions broken only by the occasional yellow patch of the peppery and mildly psychedelic flowers we use as a garnish on our food. These are the moments of beauty I live for now.

\#

The sincerity of their goodwill towards us was absolutely unquestioned. It came as such a shock to find they didn't give a fuck. They lived amongst us, the poor, with no remorse. We couldn't compete with them and we knew our fate already. Many of us chose to leave the cities and wander the land until our last days.

The new flora and fauna are amazingly nutritious so gathering food takes very little time. We occasionally cook meat on the fire but most of our diet is raw. All we need is shelter, warmth and company. We tell stories and look at the stars.

\#
\#
\#

About Walter Balerno

I grew up in Scotland where I rode my bike a lot, waited in the underpass for rain showers to end, wrote stories in school jotters, and painted pictures of my cat and other things. After deciding I had too little talent to attend art school I studied philosophy at Edinburgh University because I felt it was both interesting and unlikely to lead to a traditional job.

Here I am, writing stories and hoping that you read them.

Connect with me

Follow me on Twitter: http://twitter.com/walterbalerno

Visit my website: https://walterbalerno.com/

Or friend me on Facebook if you prefer.

Printed in Great Britain
by Amazon

72097312R00078